"You're Very Blunt, Mr. Burke."

"You're easy on the eyes. But I'm not in the market for a love affair. It's the challenge of getting your ranch out of hock that appeals to me—not seducing you."

"I'm impressed that you know me so well already," she returned, "and your modesty is refreshing! You feel that I'm so overcome with panting passion for you that I have to be warned off. I never realized I was that dangerous." Jane wiggled her eyebrows at him. "Since you're *sooo* attractive, Mr. Burke, aren't you afraid to be alone in the car with me? I might leap at you!"

"You're twisting my words."

"You're everything I've ever wanted in a man. You're handsome and intelligent and sexy. Shall we have sex right now or wait until you stop the car?"

He braked again to avoid going into the ditch. "Miss Parker!"

Dear Reader,

When *Man of the Month* began back in 1989, no one knew it would become the reader favorite it is today. Sure, we thought we were on to a good thing. After all, one of the reasons we read romance is for the great heroes! But the program was a *phenomenal* success, and now, over six years later, we are celebrating our 75th *Man of the Month*—and that's something to be proud of.

The very first *Man of the Month* was *Reluctant Father* by Diana Palmer. So who better to write the 75th *Man of the Month* than this wonderful author? In addition, this terrific story, *That Burke Man*, is also part of her LONG, TALL TEXANS series—so it's doubly special.

There are also five more great Desire books this month: *Accidental Bride* by Jackie Merritt; *One Stubborn Cowboy* by Barbara McMahon; *The Pauper and the Pregnant Princess* by Nancy Martin—which begins her OPPOSITES ATTRACT series; *Bedazzled* by Rita Rainville; and *Texas Heat* by Barbara McCauley—which begins her HEARTS OF STONE series.

This March, Desire is certainly the place to be. Enjoy!

Lucia Macro,
Senior Editor

Please address questions and book requests to:
Silhouette Reader Service
U.S.: 3010 Walden Ave., P.O. Box 1325, Buffalo, NY 14269
Canadian: P.O. Box 609, Fort Erie, Ont. L2A 5X3

DIANA PALMER
THAT BURKE MAN

SILHOUETTE *Desire*®
Published by Silhouette Books
America's Publisher of Contemporary Romance

SILHOUETTE BOOKS

ISBN 0-373-05913-2

THAT BURKE MAN

Copyright © 1995 by Diana Palmer

Printed in U.S.A.

Books by Diana Palmer

One

Todd Burke sank lower in the rickety chair at the steel rail of the rodeo arena, glowering around him from under the brim of his Stetson. He crossed one powerful blue-jeaned leg over the other and surveyed his dusty, cream-colored boots. He'd worn his dress ones for the occasion, but he'd forgotten how messy things got around livestock. It had been a long time since he'd worked on his father's ranch, and several months since Cherry's last rodeo.

The girl had a good seat for riding, but she had no self-confidence. His ex-wife didn't approve of Cherry's sudden passion for barrel racing. But he did. Cherry was all he had to show for eight years of marriage that had ended six years ago in a messy divorce. He had custody of Cherry because Marie and her new husband were too occupied with business to raise a child. Cherry was fourteen now, and a handful at times. Todd had his own worries, with a huge computer company to run and no free time. He should make more time for Cherry, but he couldn't turn over the reins of his company to subordinates. He was president and it was his job to run things.

But he was bored. The challenges were all behind him. He'd made his millions and now he was stagnating for lack of something to occupy his quick, analytical mind. He was taking a few weeks off, reluctantly, to get a new perspective on life and business during Cherry's school holidays. But he was tired of it already.

He hated sitting here while he waited for Cherry's turn to race. He and Cherry had moved to Victoria, Texas, just recently, where his new head offices were located. Jacobsville, the little town they were now in, attending the rodeo, was a nice, short drive from Victoria, and Cherry had pleaded to come, because a barrel-racing rodeo champion she idolized was supposed to accept an award of some sort here tonight. Cherry's entry in the competition had been perfunctory and resigned, because she didn't ride well before an audience and she knew it.

Her name was called and he sat up, watching his daughter lean over her horse's neck as she raced out into the arena, her pigtail flying from under her wide-brimmed hat. She looked like him, with gray eyes and fair hair. She was going to be tall, too, and she was a good rider. But when she took the first turn she hesitated and the horse slowed almost to a crawl. The announcer made a sympathetic sound, and then she did it again on the next turn.

Todd watched her ride out of the arena as her part in the competition was finished. He had a heavy heart. She'd been so hopeful, but as always, she was going to finish last.

"What a shame," came a quiet, feminine voice from down the aisle. "She just freezes on the turns, did you see? She'll never be any good as a competitor, I'm afraid. No nerve."

A male voice made a commiserating comment.

Todd, infuriated by the superiority in that female voice, waited for its owner to come into view with anger building inside him. When she did, it was a surprise.

The tall beautiful blonde who'd said those things about Cherry Burke was just complimenting herself on her steady progress. For the first time in months, Jane Parker was managing without her wheelchair or her cane. Moreover, her usual betraying limp hadn't made an appearance. Of course, she was fresh because she'd rested all day, and she hadn't strained her back. She'd been very careful not to, so that she could get through the opening ceremonies of the annual Jacobsville Rodeo and wait until its end when she was going to accept a plaque on behalf of her father. Tim had raged at her for agreeing to ride today, but it hadn't done any good. After all, she was her father's daughter. Her pride wouldn't let her ride out into the arena in a buckboard.

She stopped along the way to watch the youth competition in barrel racing. That had been her event, and she'd won trophies for it in this and other rodeos around Texas since grammar school. One particular girl caught her eye, and she commented critically on the ride—a poor one—to one of the seasoned riders leaning on the iron arena rail beside her. It was a pity that the girl hadn't finished in the money, but not surprising.

The girl was afraid of the turns and it showed in the way she choked up on the reins and hindered the horse. Jane commented on it to the cowboy. The girl must be new to rodeo, Jane thought, because her name wasn't one she knew. Here in south Texas, where she'd lived all her life, Jane knew everyone on the rodeo circuit.

She smiled at the cowboy and moved on, shaking her head. She wasn't really watching where she was going. She was trying to straighten the fringe on her rhinestone-studded white fringe jacket—which matched her long riding skirt and boots—when a big, booted foot shot across the narrow space between the trailers and slammed into the bottom metal rail of the rodeo arena, effectively freezing the elegant glittery blonde in her tracks.

Shocked, she looked down into steely gray eyes in a lean face framed by thick, fair hair.

The cowboy sitting on the trailer hitch was braiding several pieces of rawhide in his strong fingers. They didn't still, even when he spoke.

"I heard what you just said to that cowboy about Cherry Burke's ride," he said coldly. "Who the hell do you think you are to criticize a cowgirl in Cherry's class?''

She lifted both eyebrows. He wasn't a regular on the Texas circuit, either. She and her father had circled it for years. "I beg your pardon?"

"What are you, anyway, a model?" he chided. "You look like one of those blond dress-up fashion dolls in that outfit," he added as his eyes punctuated the contempt of his voice. "Are you shacking up with one of the riders or are you part of the entertainment?"

She hadn't expected a verbal attack from a total stranger. She stared at him, too surprised to react.

"Are questions of more than one syllable too hard for you?" he persisted.

That got through the surprise. Her blue eyes glittered at him. "Funny, I'd have said they're the only kind you're capable of asking," she said in her soft, cultured voice. She looked at his leg, still blocking her path. "Move it or I'll break it, cowboy."

"A cream puff like you?" he scoffed.

"That's where you're wrong. I'm no cream puff." In his position on the hitch, he was precariously balanced. She reached over, grimacing because the movement hurt her back, caught his ankle and jerked it up. He went over backward with a harsh curse.

She dusted off her hands and kept walking, aware of a wide grin from two cowboys she passed on her way to the gate.

Tim Harley, her middle-aged ranch foreman, was waiting for her by the gate with Bracket, her palomino gelding. He held the horse for her, grimacing as he watched her slow, painful ascension into the saddle.

"You shouldn't try this," he said. "It's too soon!"

"Dad would have done it," she countered. "Jacobsville was his hometown, and it's mine. I couldn't refuse the invitation to accept the plaque for Dad. Today's rodeo is dedicated to him."

"You could have accepted the plaque on foot or in a buckboard," he muttered.

She glared down at him. "Listen, I wasn't always a cripple...!"

"Oh, for God's sake!"

The sound of the band tuning up got her attention. She soothed her nervous horse, aware of angry footsteps coming along the aisle between the trailers and the arena. Fortunately, before the fair-haired cowboy got close, the other riders joined her at the gate and arranged themselves in a flanking pattern.

The youth competition marked the end of the evening's entertainment. The money for top prizes had been announced and awarded. The band began to play "The Yellow Rose of Texas." The gate opened. Jane coaxed Bracket into his elegant trot and bit down on her lower lip to contain the agony of the horse's motion. He was smooth and gaited, but even so, the jarring was painful.

She didn't know if she'd make it around that arena, but she was going to try. With a wan smile, she forced herself to look happy, to take off her white Stetson and wave to the cheering crowd. Most of these people had known her father, and a good many of them knew her. She'd been a legend in barrel racing before her forced retirement at the age of twenty-four. Her father often said that she was heaven on a horse. She tried not to think about her last sight of him. She wanted to remember him as he had been, in the time before...

"Isn't she as pretty as a picture?" Bob Harris was saying from the press booth. "Miss Jane Parker, ladies and gentlemen, two-time world's champion barrel-racer and best all around in last year's women's division. As you know, she's retired from the ring now, but she's still one magnificent sight on a horse!"

She drank in the cheers and managed not to fall off or cry out in pain when she got to the reviewing stand. It had been touch and go.

Bob Harris came out into the arena with a plaque and handed it up to her. "Don't try to get down," he said flatly, holding a hand over the microphone.

"Folks," he continued loudly, "as you know, Oren Parker was killed earlier this year in a car crash. He was best all-around four years running in this rodeo, and world's champion roper twice. I know you'll all join with me in our condolences as I dedicate this rodeo to his memory and present Jane with this plaque in honor of her father's matchless career as a top hand and a great rodeo cowboy. Miss Jane Parker, ladies and gentlemen!"

There were cheers and more applause. Jane waved the plaque and as Bob held the microphone up, she quickly thanked everyone for their kindness and for the plaque honoring her father. Then before she fell off the horse, she thanked Bob again and rode out of the arena.

She couldn't get down. That was the first real surprise of the evening. The second was to find that same angry, fair-haired cowboy standing there waiting for her to come out of the ring.

He caught her bridle and held her horse in place while he glared up at her. "Well, you sure as hell don't look the part," he said mockingly. "You ride like a raw beginner, as stiff as a board in the saddle. How did a rider as bad as you ever even get to the finals? Did you do it on *Daddy's* name?"

If she'd been hurting a little less, she was certain that she'd have put her boot right in his mouth. Sadly she was in too much pain to react.

"No spirit either, huh?" he persisted.

"Hold on, Jane, I'm coming!" came a gruff voice from behind her. "Damned fool stunt," Tim growled as he came up beside her, his gray hair and unruly beard making him look even more wizened than normal. "Can't get off, can you? Okay, Tim's here. You just come down at your own pace." He took the plaque from her.

"Does she always have to be lifted off a horse?" the stranger drawled. "I thought rodeo stars could mount and dismount all by themselves."

He didn't have a Texas accent. In fact, he didn't have much of an accent at all. She wondered where he was from.

Tim glared at him. "You won't last long on this circuit with that mouth," he told the man. "And especially not using it on Jane."

He turned back to her, holding his arms up. "Come on, pumpkin," he coaxed, in the same tone he'd used when she was only six, instead of twenty-five as she was now. "Come on. It's all right, I won't let you fall."

The new cowboy was watching with a scowl. It suddenly had occurred to him that her face was a pasty white and she was gritting her teeth as she tried to ease down. The wizened little cowboy was already straining. He was tiny, and she wasn't big, but she was tall and certainly no lightweight.

He moved forward. "Let me," he said, moving in front of Tim.

"Don't let her fall," Tim said quickly. "That back brace won't save her if you do."

"Back brace..." It certainly explained a lot. He felt it when he took her gently by the waist, the ribbing hard under his fingers. She was sweating now with the effort, and tears escaped her eyes. She closed them, shivering.

"I can't," she whispered, in agony.

"Put your arms around my neck," he said with authority. "I'll take your weight. You can slide along and I'll catch you when you've got the other foot out of the stirrup. Take it easy. Whenever you're ready."

She knew that she couldn't stay on the animal forever, but it was tempting. She managed a wan smile at Tim's worried figure. "Don't natter, Tim," she whispered hoarsely. "I've got this far. I'll get the rest of the way." She took a deep breath, set her teeth together and pulled.

The pain was excruciating. She felt it in every cell of her body before the cowboy had her carefully in his arms, clear of the ground, but she didn't whimper.

Not once. She lay there against his broad chest, shuddering with pain.

"Where do you want her?" he asked the older man.

Tim hesitated, but he knew the girl couldn't walk and he sure as hell couldn't carry her. "This way," he said after a minute, and led the tall man to a motor home several hundred yards down the line.

It was a nice little trailer, with a large sitting area. There was a sofa along one side and next to it, a wheelchair. When the cowboy saw the wheelchair, his face contorted.

"I told you," Tim was raging at her. "I told you not to do it! God knows how much you've set yourself back!"

"No...not there!" Jane protested sharply when he started to put her down in the wheelchair. "For God's sake, not there!"

"It's the best place for you, you silly woman!" Tim snapped.

"On the sofa, please," she whispered, fighting back a sharp moan as he lowered her gently to the cushions.

"I'll get your pain capsules and something to drink," Tim said, moving into the small kitchen.

"Thank you," Jane told the tall cowboy. It was a grudging thank-you, because he'd said some harsh things and she was angry.

"No need," he replied quietly. "You might have stopped me before I made a complete fool of myself. I suppose you've forgotten more about racing than Cherry will ever learn. Cherry's my daughter," he added.

That explained a lot. She grimaced as she shifted. "I'm sorry you took the criticism the wrong way, but I won't apologize for it," she said stiffly. "She's got the talent, but she's afraid of the turns. Someone needs to help her...get better control of her fears and her horse."

"I can ride, but that's about it. I don't know enough about rodeo to do her any good," he said flatly, "even though we're as crazy about rodeo in Wyoming as you Texans are."

"You're from Wyoming?" she asked, curious.

"Yes. We moved to Texas a few weeks ago, so that..." He stopped, strangely reluctant to tell her it was because he'd moved his company headquarters there to deal with an expanded market in Texas. "So that we could be closer to Cherry's mother," he amended. In fact, that hadn't influenced his decision to move to Victoria. Marie was no one's idea of a mother, and she'd been overly critical of Cherry for some time. It was a coincidence that Marie and her husband moved to Victoria from Houston about the same time Todd had moved his company headquarters there. Or so Marie said. "She and her second husband live in Victoria."

She let her eyes slide over his lean, hard face. "Does her mother ride? Couldn't she help her?"

His eyes seemed to darken. "Her mother hates horses. She didn't want Cherry in rodeo at all, but I put my foot down. Rodeo is the most important thing in Cherry's life."

"Then she should be allowed to do it," she agreed, and she was thinking how sad it was that he and his wife were divorced. His poor little girl. She knew what it was like to grow up without a mother. Her mother had died of pneumonia when she was barely in school.

She glanced back at the man. He'd said they were from Wyoming. That explained the lack of a Texas accent. She lay back, and the pain bit into her slender body like teeth. Hot tears wet her eyes as she struggled with the anguish it caused her just to move.

Tim came back and handed her two capsules and a cola. She swallowed the medicine and sipped the cold liquid, savoring the nip of it against her tongue. If only the pain would stop.

"That's sweet," she said with a sigh.

The tall man stood looking down at her with a frown. "Are you all right?"

"Sure," she said. "I'm just dandy. Thanks for your help."

She wasn't forthcoming, and he had no right to expect it. He nodded and moved out of the trailer.

Tim came after him. "Thanks for your help, stranger," he said. "I'd never have got her here by myself."

They shook hands. "My pleasure." He paused. "What happened to her?" he added abruptly.

"Her daddy wrecked the car," he said simply. "He was killed instantly, but Jane was pinned in there with him for three hours or more. They thought she'd broken her back," he concluded.

There was a harsh intake of breath.

"Oh, it was a herniated disk instead. It's painful and slow to heal, and she'll most always have some pain with it. But they can work miracles these days.

She couldn't walk right away, though, and we weren't sure if she'd be paralyzed. But she got up out of that bed and started working on herself. Stayed in physical therapy until even the doctors grinned. Never knew a girl like her," he mused. "This thing has taken some of the fight out of her, of course, but she's no quitter. Her dad would have been proud. Sad about her career, though. She'll never ride in competition again."

"What in hell was she doing on that horse this morning?"

"Showing everybody that nothing short of death will ever keep her down," Tim said simply. "Never did catch your name, stranger."

"Burke. Todd Burke."

"I'm Tim Harley. I'm proud to meet you."

"Same here." He hesitated for just a minute before he turned and went back along the aisles. He felt odd. He'd never felt so odd in his life before. Perhaps, he thought, it was that he wasn't used to proud women. She'd surprised him with the extent of her grit and stubbornness. She wasn't a quitter, in spite of impossible circumstances. He didn't doubt that she'd ride again, either, even if she didn't get back into competition. God, she was game! He was sorry he'd managed to get off on the wrong foot with her. He'd been irritated by the remarks she'd made about his daughter. Now he realized that she was trying to help, and he'd taken it the wrong way.

He was sensitive about Cherry. His daughter had taken more vicious criticism from her own mother than she was ever likely to get from a stranger. He'd overreacted. Now he was left with a case of badly bruised pride and a wounded ego. He smiled a little bitterly at his own embarrassment. He deserved it, being so cruel to a woman in that condition. It had been a long time since he'd made a mistake of such magnitude.

He wandered back down the lane to join his daughter, who was excitedly talking to one of the rodeo clowns.

"Dad, did you see her, that blond lady who accepted the plaque?" she asked when he was within earshot. "That was Jane Parker herself!"

"I saw her." He glanced at the young cowboy, who flushed and grinned at Cherry, and then quickly made himself scarce.

"I wish you wouldn't do that," Cherry said on a sigh. "Honestly, Dad, I'm fourteen!"

"And I'm an old bear. I know." He threw an affectionate arm around her. "You did fine, partner. I'm proud of you."

"Thanks! Where did you disappear to?"

"I helped your idol into her motor home," he said.

"My idol...Miss Parker?"

"The very same. She's got a bad back, that's why she doesn't ride anymore. She's game, though."

"She's the best barrel racer I ever saw," Cherry said. "I have a video of last year's rodeo and she's on it. The reason I begged to come to this rodeo was so that I could meet her, but she isn't riding this time. Gosh, I was disappointed when they said she'd retired. I didn't know she had a bad back."

"Neither did I," he murmured. He put an arm around her and hugged her close. She was precious to him, but he tended to busy himself too deeply in his work, especially in the years since her mother had walked out on them. "We haven't had much time together, have we? I'll make it up to you while we're on vacation."

"How about right now?" She grinned at him. "You could introduce me to Miss Parker."

He cleared his throat. How was he going to tell her that her idol thought he was about as low as a snake?

"She's so pretty," Cherry added without waiting for his answer. "Mother's pretty, too, but not like that." She grimaced. "Mother doesn't want me to come up next week, did she tell you?"

"Yes." He didn't add that they'd argued about it. Marie didn't spend any more time with Cherry than she had to. She'd walked out on the two of them for another man six years ago, declaring that Cherry was just too much for her to handle. It had devastated the young girl and left Todd Burke in the odd position of having to forego board meetings of his corporation to take care of his daughter. He hadn't minded, though. He was proud of the girl, and he'd encouraged her in everything she wanted to do, including rodeo. Marie had a fit over that. She didn't approve of her daughter riding rodeo, but Todd had put his foot down.

"What does she see in him?" Cherry asked, her gray eyes flashing and her blond pigtail swinging as she threw up her hands in a temper. "He's so picky about everything, especially his clothes. He doesn't like pets and he doesn't like children."

"He's brilliant. He has a national bestseller. It's number one on the *New York Times* list. It's been there for weeks," Todd replied.

"You're smart, too. And you're rich," she argued.

"Yes, but I'm not in his class. I'm a self-made man. I don't have a Harvard degree."

"Neither does he," Cherry said with a giggle. "He hasn't graduated. I heard Mama say so—not so that he could hear her, though."

He chuckled. "Never you mind. If she's happy, that's fine."

"Don't you love her anymore?" she asked.

His arm contracted. "Not the way I should to be married to her," he said honestly. "Marriage takes two people working to make each other happy. Your mother got tired of the long hours I had to spend at work."

"She got tired of me, too."

"She loves you, in her way," he replied. "Don't ever doubt that. But she and I found less in common the longer we lived together. Eventually we didn't have enough to sustain a marriage."

"You need someone to look after you," she told him. "I'll get married one day, you know, and then where will you be?"

He chuckled. "Alone."

"Sure," she agreed, "except for those women you never bring home."

He cleared his throat. "Cherry..."

"Never mind, I'm not stupid." She looked around at the dwindling crowd. "But you need someone to come home to, besides me. You work late at the office and go on business trips all over the place, and you're never home. So I can't go home, either. I want to go to school in Victoria in the fall. I hate boarding school.''

''You never told me that,'' he said, surprised.

''I didn't want to,'' she admitted reluctantly. ''But it's just awful lately. I'm glad I'm out for the summer.'' She looked up at him with gray eyes so similar to his own. ''I'm glad you took this vacation. We can do some things together, just you and me.''

''I've been thinking about it for a long time,'' he confessed. ''I'm looking forward to having a few weeks off,'' he lied convincingly, and wondered how he was going to survive the lack of anything challenging to do.

She grinned. ''Good! You can help me work on those turns in barrel racing. I don't guess you noticed, but I'm having a real hard time with them.''

He recalled what Jane Parker had said about Cherry, and he allowed himself to wonder if it might not do both women good to spend a little time talking together.

''You know,'' he mused aloud, ''I think I may have some ideas about that.''

''Really? What are they?''

''Wait and see.'' He led her toward their car. ''Let's get something to eat. I don't know about you, but I'm starved!''

''Me, too. How about Chinese?''

''My favorite.''

He put her into the old Ford he'd borrowed while his Ferrari was being serviced, and drove her back into Jacobsville.

They had lunch at the single Chinese restaurant that was nestled among half a dozen barbecue, steak and fast-food restaurants. When they finished, they went back out to the arena to watch the rest of the afternoon's competition. Cherry was only in one other event. She did poorly again, though, trying to go around the barrels. When she rode out of the arena, she was in tears.

"Now, now." Todd comforted her. "Rome wasn't built in a day."

"They didn't have barrel racing in Rome!" she wailed.

"Probably not, but the sentiment is the same." He hugged her gently. "Perk up, now. This is only the first rodeo in a whole string of them. You'll get better."

"It's a waste of time," she said, wiping her tears. "I might as well quit right now."

"Nobody ever got anywhere by quitting after one loss," he chided. "Where would I be if I'd given up when my first computer program didn't sell?"

"Not where you are today, that's for sure," she admitted. "Nobody does software like you do, Dad. That newest word processor is just radical! Everyone at school loves it. It makes term papers so easy!"

"I'm glad to hear that all those late hours we put into developing it were worth the effort," he said. He grinned at her. "We're working on a new accounting package right now."

"Oh, accounting," she muttered. "Who wants any boring old stuff like that?"

"Plenty of small businesses," he said on a chuckle. "And thank your lucky stars or we'd be in the hole."

Cherry was looking around while he spoke. Her face lit up and her eyes began to sparkle. "It's Miss Parker!" The smile faded. "Oh, my..."

He turned and the somber expression on his daughter's face was mirrored in his own. Jane was in the wheelchair, wearing jeans and a beige T-shirt and sneakers, looking fragile and depressed as Tim pushed her toward the motor home with the horse trailer hitched behind it.

Unless he missed his guess, they were about to leave. He couldn't let her get away, not before he had a chance to ask her about working with Cherry. It had occurred to him that they might kill two birds with one stone—give Miss Parker a new interest, and Cherry some badly needed help.

Two

"Miss Parker!" Todd called.

She glanced in his direction, aware that he and a young girl with fair hair in a pigtail were moving toward her. The wheelchair made her feel vulnerable and she bit down hard on her lip. She was in a bad temper because she didn't want that rude, unpleasant man to see her this way.

"Yes?" she asked through her teeth.

"This is my daughter, Cherry," he said, pulling the young girl forward. "She wanted to meet you."

Regardless, apparently, of whether Jane wanted the meeting or not. "How do you do," she said through numb lips.

"What happened to you?" Cherry spluttered.

Jane's face contorted.

"She was in a wreck," her father said shortly, "and it was rude of you to ask."

Cherry flushed. "I'm sorry, really I am." She went to the wheelchair, totally uninhibited, and squatted beside it. "I've watched all the videos you were on. You were just the best in the world," she said enthusiastically. "I couldn't get to the rodeos, but I had Dad buy me the videos from people who taped the events. I'm having a lot of trouble on the turns. Dad can ride, but he's just hopeless on rodeo, aren't you, Dad?" She put a gentle hand over Jane's arm. "Will you be able to ride again?"

"Cherry!" Todd raged.

"It's all right," Jane said quietly. She looked into the girl's clear, gray eyes, seeing no pity there, only honest concern and curiosity. The rigidity in her began to subside. She smiled. "No," she said honestly. "I don't think I'll be able to ride again. Not in competition, at least."

"I wish I could help you," Cherry said. "I'm going to be a surgeon when I grow up. I make straight A's in science and math, and Dad's already said I could go to Johns Hopkins when I'm old enough. That's the best school of medicine anywhere!"

"A surgeon," Jane echoed, surprised. She smiled. "I've never known anyone who wanted to be a surgeon before."

Cherry beamed. "Now you do. I wish you didn't have to leave so soon," she said wistfully. "I was going to pick your brain for ways to get over this fear of turns. Silly, isn't it, when the sight of blood doesn't bother me at all."

Jane was aware of an emptiness in herself as she stared into the young face. It was like seeing herself at that age. She lowered her eyes. "Yes, well, I'm sorry, but it's been a long day and I'm in a good deal of pain. And we're interviewing today."

"Interviewing?" Cherry asked with open curiosity.

"For a business manager," Jane said sadly, glancing at Tim, who winced. "Tim can't manage the books. He's willing to keep on as foreman, but we're losing money hand over fist since Dad's death because neither one of us can handle the books."

"Gosh, my dad would be perfect for that," Cherry said innocently. "He's a wizard with money. He keeps the books for his compu—"

"For the small computer company I work for in Victoria," Todd said quickly, with a speaking glance that his intelligent daughter interpreted immediately. She shut up, grinning.

Tim stepped forward. "Can you balance books?"

"Sure."

Tim looked at Jane. "There's the foreman's cabin empty, since Meg and I are living in the house with you," he remarked. "They could live there. And you could help the girl with her turns. It would give you something to do besides brooding around the house all day."

"Tim!" Jane burst out angrily. She glanced apprehensively at Todd Burke, who was watching her with unconcealed amusement. "I'm sure he has a job already."

"I do. Keeping books for my . . . the computer company," he lied. "But it doesn't take up all my time. In fact, I think I'd enjoy doing something different for a while." He pursed his lips. "If you're interested, that is," he added with practiced indifference.

Jane's eyes fell to her lap.

"I'd love to learn how to win at barrel racing," Cherry said with a sigh. "I guess I'll have to give it up, though. I mean, I'm so bad that it's a waste of Dad's money to keep paying my entrance fees and all."

Jane glowered at her. She glowered at him, too, standing there like a movie cowboy with his firm lips pursed and his steely gray eyes twinkling with amusement. Laughing at her.

"She won't hire you," Tim said with a glare at her. "She's too proud to admit that you're just what she needs. She'd rather let the ranch go under while she sits on the porch and feels sorry for herself."

"Damn you!" She spat the words at Tim.

He chuckled. "See them eyes?" he asked Todd. "Like wet sapphires. She may look like a fashion doll, but she's all fur and claws when things get next to her, and she's no quitter."

Todd was looking at her with evident appreciation. He grinned. "Two week trial?" he asked. "While we see how well we all get along? I can't do you much damage in that short a time, and I might do you a lot of good. I have a way with balance sheets."

"We couldn't be much worse off," Tim reminded his boss.

Jane was silently weighing pros and cons. He had a daughter, so he had to be settled and fairly dependable, if Cherry was any indication. If she hired anyone else, she'd have no idea if she was giving succor to a thief or even a murderer. This man looked trust-worthy and his daughter apparently adored him.

"We could try, I suppose," she said finally. "If you're willing. But the ranch isn't successful enough that I can offer you much of a salary." She named a figure. "You'll get meals and board free, but I'll understand if that isn't enough—"

"If I can keep on doing my present job, in the evenings, we'll manage," Todd said without daring to look at his daughter. If he did, he knew he'd give the show away.

"Your boss won't mind?" Jane asked.

He cleared his throat. "He's very understanding. After all, I'm a single parent."

She nodded, convinced. "All right, then. Would you like to follow us out to the ranch, if you're through for the day?"

"We're through, all right," Cherry said on a sigh. "I'm dejected, demoralized and thoroughly depressed."

"Don't be silly," Jane said gently, and with a smile. "You've got an excellent seat, and you're good with horses. You just need to get over that irrational fear that you're going to go down on the turns."

"How did you know?" Cherry gasped.

"Because I was exactly the same when I started out. Stop worrying. I'll work with you. When we're through, you'll be taking home trophies."

"Really?"

Jane chuckled. "Really. Let's go, Tim."

He wheeled her to the cab of the motor home and opened the door. "I guess bringing this thing ten miles looks odd," Tim murmured to Todd, "but we had to have a place where Jane could rest. We've carried this old thing to many a rodeo over the years. She takes a little coaxing sometimes, but she always goes."

"Like Bracket," Jane mused, glancing back to the trailer where her palomino gelding rode.

"Like Bracket," Tim agreed. He reached down. "Let's get you inside, now, Jane."

Before he could lift her, Todd moved forward. "Here," he volunteered. "I'll do the honors."

Tim grinned, his relief all too obvious. Jane wasn't heavy, but Tim was feeling his age a bit.

Todd lifted Jane gently out of the wheelchair and into the cab of the big vehicle, positioning her on the seat with a minimum of discomfort. She eased her arms from around his neck a little self-consciously and smiled. "Thanks."

He shrugged powerful shoulders and smiled back. "No problem. Where does the chair go, Tim?"

He folded it and the older man climbed up into the motor home and stowed it away. He got behind the wheel and paused long enough to give directions to Todd about where in Jacobsville the ranch was located before he and Jane waved goodbye and drove away.

"Dad!" Cherry laughed. "Are we really going to do it? What will she say when she finds out?"

"We'll worry about that when the time comes. The ranch budget sounds like a challenge, and you could use some pointers with your riding," he added. "I think it may work out very well."

"But what about your company?" Cherry asked.

"I've got good people working for me and I'm on holiday." He ruffled her hair. "We'll think of it as summer vacation," he assured her. "It will give us some time together."

"I'd like that," she said solemnly. "After all, in four years I'll be in school, and you probably won't get to see me twice a year. I'll have to study very hard."

"You're smart. You'll do fine."

"Yes, I will," she assured him with a grin. "And you can have all your medical care free."

"I can hardly wait."

"Don't be sarcastic," she chided. "And you have to be nice to Miss Parker, too."

"She doesn't like me very much."

"You don't like her, either, do you?" she asked curiously.

He stuck his hands into his pockets and frowned. "She's all right."

"If you don't like her, why are you going to help her?"

He couldn't answer that. He didn't know why. She was a woman in a wheelchair, who looked as if in her heyday she'd been nothing more than a fashion doll on a horse. But she was crippled and in bad financial circumstances, and all alone, apparently. He felt sorry for her. Funny, that, because since his failed marriage, he didn't like women very much except when he had an overwhelming desire for someone female in his arms. Loving and leaving wouldn't be possible with Jane Parker. So why was he going out of his way to help her? He didn't know.

"Maybe I feel sorry for her," he told Cherry finally.

"Yes, so do I, but we mustn't let her know it," she said firmly. "She's very proud, did you notice?"

He nodded. "Proud and hot tempered."

"What familiar traits."

He glowered at her, but she just grinned.

At the luxurious house Todd had bought in Victoria, they packed up what gear they'd need for a few days, explained their forthcoming absence to their puzzled housekeeper, Rosa, promised to be back soon and drove in the borrowed Ford down to Jacobsville to the Parker ranch.

It wasn't much to look at from the road. There was a rickety gray wood and barbed-wire fence that had been mended just enough to hold in the mixed-breed steers in the pasture. The barn was still standing, but barely. The dirt road that led past a windmill to the house had potholes with water standing in them from the last rain. It had no gravel on it, and it looked as if it hadn't been graded in years. The yard was bare except for a few rosebushes and a handful of flowers around the long porch of the white clapboard house. It was two stories high, and needed painting. One of the steps had broken through and hadn't been replaced. There was a rickety ramp, presumably constructed hastily for the wheelchair, on the end of the porch. There was the motor home and horse trailer in the yard, next to a building that might be used as a garage by an optimist. A small cabin was nestled in high grass that needed cutting; the foreman's cabin,

Todd thought, hoping that it was more than one room. Nearby was a bigger structure, a small one-story house. It was in better condition and it had rocking chairs on the porch. The bunkhouse?

"Welcome!" Tim called, coming out to meet them.

They got out and Todd shook hands with him. "Thanks. If you'll tell me where to put our stuff...?" He was looking toward the cabin.

"Oh, that's where old man Hughes lives." Tim chuckled. "He helps me look after the livestock. He can't do a lot, but he's worked here since he was a boy. We can't pension him off until he's sixty-five, two more years yet." He turned. "Here's where you and the girl will bunk down." He led them toward the small house and Todd heaved a sigh of relief.

"It needs some work, like everything else, but maybe you can manage. You can have meals with us in the house. There are three other hands who mend fences and look after the tanks and the machinery, do the planting and so forth. They're mostly part-time these days, but we hire on extra men when we need them, seasonally, you know."

The house wasn't bad. It had three big bedrooms and a small living room. There was a kitchen, too, but it didn't look used. There was a coffeepot and a small stove and refrigerator.

"I could learn to cook," Cherry began.

"No, you couldn't," Todd said shortly. "Time enough for that later."

"My wife Meg'll teach you if you want to learn," Tim said, volunteering his wife with a grin. "She likes young people. Never had any kids of our own, so she takes up with other people's. When you've settled, come on over to the house. We'll have sandwiches and something to drink.''

"How's Miss Parker?'' Cherry asked.

Tim grimaced. "Lying down. She's not well. I've called the doctor.'' He shook his head. "I told her not to get on that horse, but she wouldn't listen to me. Never could do anything with her, even when she was a youngster. It took her papa to hold her back, but he's gone now.''

"She had no business on that horse,'' Todd said, pointedly.

"That was a bad attack of pride,'' Tim told him. "Some newspaperman wrote a column about the rodeo and mentioned that poor Jane Parker would probably come out to accept the plaque for her father in a wheelchair, because she was crippled now.''

Todd's face hardened. "Which paper was it in?''

"That little weekly they publish in Jacobsville,'' he said with a grimace. "She took it to heart. I told her it was probably that Sikes kid who just started doing sports. He's fresh out of journalism school and fancies himself winning a Pulitzer for covering barrel racing. Huh!'' he scoffed.

Todd mentally stored the name for future reference. "Will the doctor come out?''

"Sure!'' the wizened little man assured him. "His dad was Jane's godfather. They're great friends. He has an assistant now, though—a female doctor named Lou. She might come instead.'' He chuckled. "They don't see eye to eye on anything. Amazing how they manage a practice between them.''

"The doctor isn't married?"

He shook his head. "He was sweet on Jane, but after the accident, she cut him dead if he so much as smiled at her. That was just before Lou went into practice with him. Jane doesn't want to get involved, she says."

"She won't always be in that chair," Todd murmured as they walked toward the house.

"No. But she'll always have pain when she overdoes things, and she won't ride well enough for competition again."

"That's what she told Cherry."

Tim gave him a wary glance. "You won't hurt her?" he asked bluntly.

Todd smiled. "She's very attractive, and I like her spirit, but I've had a bad marriage and I don't want to risk another failure. I don't get serious about women anymore. And I'm not coldhearted enough to play around with Jane."

Tim sighed. "Thanks. I needed to hear that. She's more vulnerable than she realizes right now. I'm not related to her, but in a lot of ways, I'm the only family she's got—well, Meg and me."

"She's a lucky woman," Todd replied.

He shrugged. "Not so lucky, or she wouldn't be in that chair, would she?"

They walked up onto the porch, avoiding the broken step. "Meant to fix that, but I never get time," Tim murmured. "Now that you're here to tear your hair out over the books, maybe I'll be able to get a few odds and ends done."

"I can help, if you need me," he volunteered. "I do woodwork for a hobby."

"Do you!" Tim's face brightened. "There's a woodworking shop in the back of the barn. We built it years ago for her dad. He made all the furniture in the house. She'll like having it in use again."

"Are you sure?" he asked doubtfully.

"You can always ask her."

They walked into the living room. Jane was lying on the sofa, putting up a brave front even though her face was stark white with the effort. Cherry was curled up in an armchair beside the sofa, her cheek on her folded arms, listening raptly to her idol.

"Doctor should be here soon," Tim told Jane. He paused to pat her gently on the shoulder. "Hang on, kid."

She smiled at him, and laid her hand briefly over the one on her shoulder. "Thanks, Tim. What would I do without you?"

"Let's agree never to find out," he returned dryly.

"Okay." She glanced toward Todd Burke. The expression on his lean face made her angry. "I'm not a cripple," she said belligerently.

He knelt by the sofa and pushed back a strand of her hair. It was wet, not with sweat, but with tears she'd shed involuntarily as the pain bit into her. He felt more protective about her than he could understand.

"Don't you have something to take?"

"Yes," she said, shaken by his concern. "But it isn't working."

He tucked the strand of hair behind her small, pretty ear and smiled. "Guess why?"

She made a face. "I wouldn't have tried to ride out into the arena if it hadn't been for that damned reporter," she said gruffly. "He called me a cripple!"

"Cherry and I will rush right in to town and beat the stuffing out of him for you."

That brought a pained smile to her face. "Cover him in ink and wrap him up in his newspaper and hang him from a printing press."

"They don't have printing presses anymore," Cherry said knowledgeably. "Everything's cold type now... offset printing."

Jane's blue eyes widened. "My, my, you are a well-spring of information!" she said, impressed.

Cherry grinned smugly. "One of my new teachers used to work for a newspaper. Now he teaches English."

"She knows everything," Todd said with a resigned air. "Just ask her."

"Not *everything*, Dad." She chuckled. "I don't know how to do barrel-racing turns."

"I hear a car," Tim said, glancing out the window. "It's him."

Todd frowned at the way Jane's eyes fell when he looked into them. Did she have mixed feelings about the doctor and was trying to hide it? Maybe Tim had been wrong and Jane had been sweet on the doctor, not the other way around.

Todd got to his feet as a tall man with red hair came into the room, carrying a black bag. He was dressed in a nice gray Western-cut suit with a white shirt and a black string tie. Boots, too. He removed a pearl gray Stetson from his head, and tossed it onto the counter.

Pale blue eyes swept the room, lingering on Todd Burke, who stared back, unsmiling.

"This is Dr. Jebediah Coltrain," Tim introduced the tall, slim man. "When he was younger, everybody used to call him Copper."

"They don't anymore. Not without a head start," the doctor said. He didn't smile, either.

"This is Todd Burke and his daughter Cherry," Tim said, introducing them. "Todd's going to take over the book work for us."

Coltrain didn't say much. He gave Todd a piercing stare that all but impaled him before he nodded curtly, without offering a hand in greeting. He was less reserved with Cherry, if that faint upturn of his thin lips was actually a smile.

"Well, what fool thing have you done this time?" Coltrain asked Jane irritably. "Gone riding, I guess?"

She glared at him through waves of pain. "I wasn't going to let them push me out into that arena in a wheelchair," she said furiously. "Not after what that weasel of a sports reporter wrote about me!"

He made a sound deep in his throat that could have meant anything. He set about examining her with steely hands that looked menacing until they touched and probed with a tenderness that set Todd's teeth on edge.

"Muscle strain," Coltrain pronounced at last. "You'll need a few days in bed on muscle relaxers. Did you rent that traction rig I told you to get?"

"Yes, we did, under protest," Tim said with a chuckle.

"Well, get started, then."

He lifted her as if she were a feather and carried her off to her bedroom. Todd, incensed out of all reason, followed them with an audible tread.

Coltrain glanced over his shoulder at the other man with a faintly mocking smile. He didn't need a road map to find a marked trail, and he knew jealousy when he saw it.

He put Jane down gently on the double bed with its carved posts with the traction apparatus poised over it.

"Need to make a pit stop before I hook you up?" Coltrain asked her without a trace of embarrassment.

"No, I'm fine," she said through clenched teeth. "Go ahead."

He adjusted the brace that lifted her right leg, putting a pleasant pressure on the damaged hip that even surgery hadn't put completely back to rights. "This won't work any miracles, but it will help," Coltrain told her. "You put too much stock in articles written by idiots."

"He didn't write it about you!"

He lifted an eyebrow. "He wouldn't dare," he said simply.

She knew that. It irritated her. She closed her eyes. "It hurts."

"I can do something for that." Coltrain reached in his bag and drew out a small bottle and a syringe. He handed a package to Todd. "Open that and swab the top of the bottle with it."

He had the sort of voice that expects obedience. Todd, who never took orders, actually did it with only a lopsided grin. He liked the doctor, against his will.

Coltrain upended the bottle when Todd had finished, inserted the needle into the bottle and then drew up the correct amount of painkiller.

He handed Todd another package containing an alcohol-soaked gauze. "Swab her arm, here."

He indicated a vein in her right arm and Todd looked at him.

"It's not addictive," the doctor said gently. "I know what I'm doing."

Todd made a rough murmur and complied. It embarrassed him to show concern for a woman he barely knew. Coltrain's knowing look made it worse.

He swabbed her arm and Coltrain shot the needle in, efficiently and with a minimum of pain.

"Thanks, Copper," Jane told him quietly.

He shrugged. "What are friends for?" He took a few sample packages out of the bag and gave them to Todd. "Two every six hours for severe pain. They're stronger than the others I gave you," he told Jane. "You can push this to five hours if you can't bear it, but no sooner." Coltrain fastened his bag and gave Jane a reassuring smile. "Stay put. I'll check on you tomorrow."

"Okay." Her eyes were already closing.

"I'll sit with you until you go to sleep," Cherry volunteered, and Jane smiled her agreement.

Coltrain jerked his head toward the living room. Tim and Todd followed. He closed the bedroom door behind them.

"I want her X-rayed," he told them without preamble. "I think it's muscular, but I'm not going to stake my life on it. The last thing she needed was to get on a horse."

"I tried to stop her," Tim told him.

"I realize that. I'm not blaming you. She's a handful." He eyed Todd openly. "Can you keep her off horses?"

Todd smiled slowly. "Watch me."

"That's what I thought. She isn't safe to be let out alone these days, always trying to prove herself." He grabbed his Stetson and started toward the door. "She's in too much pain to be moved today. I'll send an ambulance for her in the morning and make all the necessary arrangements at Jacobsville Memorial. She won't like it," he added wryly.

"But she'll do it," Todd replied easily.

For the first time, Coltrain chuckled. "I'd like to be a fly on the wall tomorrow when that ambulance gets here."

The telephone rang and Tim answered it. He grimaced, holding it out to Coltrain.

The other man picked it up with a rough sigh. "Coltrain," he said as if he knew who was calling.

His face grew harder by the second. "Yes. No. I don't give a damn, it's my practice and that's how I do things. If you don't like it, get out. Damn the contract!" He glanced at the wide-eyed faces near him and shifted his posture. "We'll talk about this when I get back. Yes, you do that." He put the receiver down with a savagely controlled jerk of his lean hand. His eyes glittered like blue water on a snake's back. "Call me if you need me."

After he was gone, and was driving away in a cloud of dust, Tim whistled through his teeth. "It won't last."

"What won't?" Todd replied.

"Him and Lou," he said, shaking his head. "They'll kill each other one day, him with his old-fashioned way of practicing and her with all this new-fangled technology."

Todd found himself vaguely relieved that the doctor had someone besides Jane to occupy his mind. He wasn't sure why, but he didn't like the tenderness Coltrain had shown Jane.

Three

Jane was restless all through the night. When Cherry went to bed, Todd sat with Jane. Tim had handed over the books earlier, so he took the heavy ledger with him. He looked through it while Jane slept, his reading glasses perched on his straight nose and a scowl between his eyes as he saw the inefficiency and waste there on the paper.

The ranch had almost gone under, all right, and there was no need. In addition to the beef cattle, Jane had four thoroughbred stallions, two of whom had won ribbons in competition, and on the racetrack before her father's death. She wasn't even putting them at stud, which could certainly have added to the coffers. The equipment she was using was obsolete. No maintenance had been done recently, either, and that would have made a handsome tax deduction. From what he'd seen, there was plenty of room for improvement in the equipment shed, the outbuildings, the barn and even the house itself. The ranch had great potential, but it wasn't being efficiently used.

He scowled, faintly aware of a tingling sensation, as if he were being watched. He lifted his head and looked into curious blue eyes.

"I didn't know you wore glasses," Jane said drowsily.

"I'm farsighted," he said with a chuckle. "It's irritating when people think I'm over forty because of these." He touched the glasses.

She studied his lean, hard face quietly. "How old are you?"

"Thirty-five," he said. "You?"

She grinned. "Twenty-five. A mere child, compared to you."

He lifted an eyebrow. "You must be feeling better."

"A little." She took a slow breath. "I hate being helpless."

"You won't always be," he reminded her. "One day, you won't have to worry about traction and pills. Try to think of this as a temporary setback."

"I'll bet you've never been helpless in your whole life."

"I had pneumonia once," he recalled. His face hardened with memory. He'd been violently ill, because he hadn't realized how serious his chest cold had become until his fever shot up and he couldn't walk for pain and lack of breath. The doctor had reluctantly allowed him to stay at home during treatment, with the proviso that he had to be carefully watched. But Marie had left him alone to go to a cocktail party with his best friend, smiling as she swept out the door. After all, it was just a little cough and he'd be fine, she'd said carelessly. Besides, this party was important to her. She was going to meet several society matrons who were potential clients for her new interior-design business. She couldn't pass that up. It wasn't as if pneumonia was even serious, she'd laughed lightly on her way out the door.

"Come back," Jane said softly.

His head jerked as he realized his thoughts had drifted away. "Sorry."

"What happened?" she persisted.

He shrugged. "Nothing much. I had pneumonia and my wife left me at home to go to a cocktail party."

"And?" she persisted.

"You're as stubborn as a bulldog, aren't you?" he asked irritably. "You're prying."

"Of course I am," she said easily. "Tell me."

"She went on to an all-night club after the cocktail party and didn't come home until late the next morning. She'd put my antibiotics away and hadn't told me where, and I was too sick to get up and look for them. By the time she got home, I was delirious with fever. She had to get an ambulance and rush me to the hospital. I very nearly died. That was the year Cherry was born."

"Why, the witch!" Jane said bluntly. "And you stayed with her?"

"Cherry was on the way," he said starkly. "I knew that if we got divorced, she wouldn't have the baby. I wanted Cherry," he said stiffly.

He said it as if it embarrassed him, and that made her smile. "I've noticed that you take fatherhood seriously."

"I always wanted kids," he said. "I was an only child. It's a lonely life for a kid on a big ranch. I wanted more than one, but..." He shrugged. "I'm glad I've got Cherry."

"Her mother didn't want her?"

He glowered. "Marie likes her when she's having guests, so that she can show the world what a sweet, devoted mother she is. It wins her brownie points in her business affairs. She's an interior designer and most of her work comes from very wealthy, very conservative, Texans. You know, the sort who like settled family men and women on the job?"

"Does Cherry know?"

"It's hard to miss, and Cherry's bright. Marie and I get along, most of the time, but I won't let her dictate Cherry's life for her." He intercepted a curious glance. "Rodeo," he said, answering the unspoken question. "Marie disapproves."

"But Cherry still rides."

He nodded. "I have custody," he said pointedly.

"And Cherry adores you," she agreed. She smiled, still drowsy from the pain medication. "I feel as if I'm flying. I don't know what Copper gave me, but it's very potent."

"Coltrain strikes me as something of a hell-raiser," he said.

"He was, and still is. I like him very much."

One gray eye narrowed. "Like?"

"Like." She was fighting sleep. Her slender hands smoothed over the light sheet that covered her. "I wanted to care about him, at first, but I couldn't feel like that with him. I think I'm cold, you see," she murmured sleepily. "I don't...feel those things...that women are supposed to feel...with men..."

Her voice drifted away and she was asleep.

Todd sat watching her with a faint frown, puzzled by that odd statement. She was a beauty. Surely there had been men over the years who attracted her, and at least one lover; perhaps Coltrain, for whom she hadn't felt anything. The thought was uncomfortable.

After a minute, he forced himself to concentrate more on the figures in the ledger and less on the lovely, sleeping woman in the bed. Jane's sex life was none of his business.

The ambulance came promptly at ten o'clock the next morning, and Jane's blue eyes snapped and sparkled when Todd told her that Coltrain had insisted on an X ray.

"I won't go!" she raged. "Do you hear me? I won't go to the hospital...!"

"He only wants you X-rayed to be sure that you haven't broken anything," Todd said. He was alone in the bedroom with Jane. Tim had prudently found something to do several miles away from the house, and Meg had gone shopping, taking Cherry with her. Only now did Todd realize why.

"I haven't broken anything!" she said hotly. She'd already had the traction apparatus removed so that she could go to the bathroom. Now she was sitting on the side of the bed in her pale blue cotton pajamas, her blond hair disheveled around her shoulders while she glared at the men who brought in the trolley.

"I won't go!" she continued.

The ambulance attendants looked doubtful.

Jane waved a hand at them. "Take that thing away!"

"Stay right where you are," Todd said quietly. He moved toward Jane. "Coltrain said you go. So you go."

She verbally lashed out at him, furious that she was being coerced into doing this. "I tell you, I won't...!"

He ignored her words and simply picked her up, cradling her gently against his broad chest as he turned toward the stretcher. She felt her breasts flatten against that warm strength and something incredible happened to her senses. She gasped audibly at the sensations that rippled through her slender body at the unfamiliar contact. Until now, the only man who'd ever seen her so scantily clad had been Coltrain, in a professional capacity only. And now here she was in arms that made a weakling of her, that made her whole body tingle and tremble with odd, empty longings.

All too soon, Todd put her on the stretcher and the ambulance attendants covered her with a white sheet. They were quick and professional, towing her right out toward the ambulance, which had backed up to the porch and was waiting for her.

"I'll follow you in the car," Todd told her. The way she was watching him made him uneasy. He couldn't help feeling her violent reaction to his touch. It had been in her whole body, even as it lay in her eyes right now, surprised and vulnerable eyes that made him very uncomfortable. "What, no more harsh words? No more fury?" he taunted, hoping to stop those soft eyes from eating his face.

Her teeth clenched, as much from physical discomfort as temper. "You're fired!" she yelled at him.

"Oh, you can't fire me," he assured her.

"Why can't I?"

"Because you'll lose the ranch if you do," he said, meeting her angry eyes levelly. "I can save it."

She wavered. "How?"

"We'll discuss that. After you're X-rayed," he added. He moved back and the ambulance attendant closed the double doors on Jane and her confused expression.

"I told you I was all right!" Jane raged at Coltrain when he'd read the X rays and assured her that nothing was broken, chipped or fractured.

"I didn't say you were all right," he returned, his hands deep in the pockets of his white lab coat. He looked very professional with the stethoscope draped loosely around his neck. "I said you hadn't broken anything. You were lucky," he added irritably. "My God, woman, do you want to break your back? Do you want to spend the rest of your life lying in bed, unable to move!"

She bit her lower lip hard. "No," she said gruffly.

"Then stop trying to prove yourself," he said shortly. "The only opinion that ever matters is your own! Damn the reporter. If he's too stupid to report the truth, he'll dig his own grave one day. If he hasn't already," he added.

"What do you mean?"

"I mean that the local rodeo association has banned him from the arena," he told her.

Her eyebrows shot up. "But rodeo is the biggest local sport going, especially this time of year!"

"I know." He smiled smugly. "I sit on the board of directors."

"You did it," she said.

"I had a lot of help," he replied. "It was a unanimous decision. I wish you could have seen Craig Fox's face when he was told he couldn't send his new reporter to cover any more rodeos." He fingered his tie. "As a matter of fact, the hardware store and the auto parts place pulled their ads this week. Their owners have sons who compete in the rodeo."

She whistled through her teeth. "Oh, boy."

"I understand that the reporter is making a public apology, in print, in this week's edition," he added. "You, uh, might take a look on the editorial page when your copy comes." He patted her shoulder absently. "He eats crow very well."

She laughed, her bad temper gone. "You devil!"

"You're my friend," he said with a smile—something rare in that taciturn face.

"And you're mine." She reached out and held his lean hand. "Thanks, Copper."

He nodded.

Todd Burke, coming into the treatment room with Dr. Lou Blakely, stopped and glared at the tableau they made. The lovely blond woman beside him didn't give away anything in her expression, but her eyelids flickered.

"When you're through here, I'd like to speak to you, Dr. Coltrain," Lou said quietly. "I had Ned Rogers come in for some lab work. It isn't good, I'm afraid. I let him go home, but we'll have to have him back to give him the results."

He let go of Jane's hand, reluctantly it seemed to Todd, and turned to his partner. "Was it so urgent that you couldn't tell me after I'd done my rounds here?" he asked shortly. "Who's minding the office?"

Her cheeks flushed. "I've just finished doing my own rounds," she said, furious that he thought she was chasing him here. "And it *is* noon," she said pointedly. "I'm on my lunch hour. Betty's had her lunch. She's minding the phone."

"Noon?" He checked his watch. "So it is." He turned toward Jane and started to speak.

"I'll drive Jane back home, if she's through here," Todd interjected, joining them. "I have some questions about the book work. I can't do anything more until they're answered."

Lou studied the newcomer curiously and with a nice smile. "I'm Dr. Louise Blakely," she said, holding a hand out to be shaken. "Dr. Coltrain's partner."

"Assistant," Coltrain said carelessly, and with a pointed glare. There was no interest in his eyes, no curiosity, nothing except a faint glitter of hostility.

"Todd Burke," Todd introduced himself, and smiled. "Nice to meet you, Dr. Blakely."

Lou glanced at Coltrain. "The contract I signed says that we're partners, Dr. Coltrain," she persisted. "For a year."

He didn't reply. His pale eyes went back to Jane and he smiled. "I'll be around if you need me. Take it easy, okay?"

Jane smiled back. "Okay."

He patted her shoulder reassuringly and started for the door. "All right," he told Lou curtly. "Let's have a look at Mr. Rogers's test results."

Todd watched them go before he helped Jane into the wheelchair the nurse had brought into the room. She was wheeled out to the exit and Todd loaded her into his Ford. They were underway before he spoke.

"Are you jealous of Lou?" he asked abruptly, because he'd seen the way she watched Coltrain and Lou Blakely.

"Because of Copper? No," she said easily. "I was wondering about Lou. She's...I don't know...fragile around him. It's odd, because she's such a strong, independent woman most of the time."

"Maybe she's sweet on him," he suggested.

"For her sake, I hope not," she replied. "Copper is a confirmed bachelor. His work is his whole life, and he likes women but only in numbers."

Todd smiled faintly.

She glanced at him with twinkling eyes. "I see that you understand the way he feels. That's the way you are, too, isn't it?"

He nodded. "A man who's been burned doesn't go around looking for fires," he said pointedly. He braked for a traffic light and then pulled out into the road that led out of Jacobsville toward the Parker ranch.

She stared out at the summer landscape as they left town, smiling at the beauty of flowers and crops in the field. "I can understand why you might feel that way," she said absently.

"I'm glad," he replied curtly, "because there was a look in your eyes that worried me when I lifted you onto the stretcher back at the house."

Her eyebrows raised. "You're blunt," she said.

"Yes, I am. I've found that it's easier to be honest than to prevaricate." His hands tightened on the steering wheel. "You're easy on the eyes and I think I'll enjoy working for you. But I'm not in the market for a love affair. It's the challenge of getting your ranch out of hock that appeals to me—not seducing you."

She didn't react visibly. She folded her arms over her breasts lazily and leaned back against the seat. It didn't show that she felt cold and empty and wounded inside. "I see."

"And now you're offended," he said with a cutting edge to his voice, "and you'll pout for the rest of the day."

She laughed. "I'm impressed that you know me so well already, Mr. Burke," she returned. "And your modesty is refreshing!"

His brows collided. He hadn't expected that mocking reply. "I beg your pardon?"

"You feel that I'm so overcome with panting passion for you that I have to be warned off. I never realized I was that dangerous. And in a wheelchair, too." She wiggled her eyebrows at him. "Since you're *sooooo* attractive, Mr. Burke, aren't you afraid to be alone in the car with me? I might leap on you!"

He was disconcerted. He glanced at her and the car swerved. He muttered under his breath as he righted it in his lane.

Jane began to enjoy herself. He didn't seem the sort of man who was easily rattled. She'd managed that quite nicely. She couldn't wait to do it again. Two could play at his game.

"You're making me sound conceited," he began.

"Really? Well, you do seem to think that no normal woman can resist you."

He sighed angrily. "You're twisting my words."

"I do find you attractive," she said. "You're everything I've ever wanted in a man. I think you're handsome and intelligent and sexy. Shall we just have sex right now or wait until you stop the car?"

The car swerved again and he braked to avoid going into the ditch. "Miss Parker!"

She was enjoying herself. For the first time since the wreck, she could laugh. She had to fight to get herself under control at all.

"Oh, I'm sorry," she said when she got a glimpse at his hard features. "Really, I am."

He pulled onto the ranch road, his teeth clenched. She made him out to be an utter fool, and he didn't like it. He wasn't used to women who were that good at verbal repartee. Marie was sarcastic and biting at times, but she was never condescending. Jane Parker was another kettle of fish. He had to remember that her body was fragile, even if her ego wasn't.

"I haven't laughed like that in months," she said, calmer when he pulled up at the front door. "I do apologize, but it felt good to laugh."

He cut off the ignition and turned in the seat to face her. His eyes glittered, as they had at their first meeting. He was trying to control emotions he'd never felt to such an extent.

"I don't like being the butt of anyone's joke," he said curtly. "We'll get along very well if you remember that."

Her eyes iced over. "We'll get along better if you remember that I don't like men who talk to me as if I were a giddy adolescent on a hero-worshiping tangent."

His jaw clenched. "Miss Parker, I'm no boy. And I do know how a woman reacts—"

"No doubt you do, with your wide experience of them." She cut him off. "I've been alone for some time now," she added, "and I'm not used to being touched. So before you read too much into my reactions, you might consider that any man would have produced the same reaction."

He didn't like that. His expression went from surprise to cold courtesy. "I'll get you into the house."

"No, you won't," she said pleasantly. The look in her eyes wasn't pleasant at all. "Please ask Tim to bring the wheelchair. I find that I prefer it to you."

His face registered the insult. He knew already how she hated the stigma of the chair. But he didn't react. He should have kept his mouth shut.

"I'll get it," he said.

He left her in the car and went into the house, fuming. Tim came out of the kitchen where he'd been talking to Meg.

"How is she?" he asked at once.

"Out of humor, but physically undamaged," Todd said. He grimaced. "I made her mad."

"That's a step in the right direction," the older man said, smiling. "She needs shaking up. Pity she doesn't like Copper," he added on a sigh. "He'd be perfect for her."

"Because he's a doctor?" Todd asked impatiently.

"Because they grew up together and he knows ranching," came the reply. "He'd never have let the place get in this mess." He eyed Todd narrowly. "Do you think you can get us out of the financial tangle I landed us in?"

Todd reached for the wheelchair. "I think so," he said. "It's not as bad as you think. Mainly it's a matter of improving the operation and utilizing some resources. It will take time, though," he added as he pushed the chair toward the porch. "Don't expect instant answers."

"I don't," Tim assured him. "Why can't you just carry her inside?" he asked as an afterthought.

"Never mind." Todd bit off the words.

Tim's eyes twinkled. He followed the younger man out to the car and watched the byplay as Todd eased Jane into the chair and pushed her up onto the porch.

She was stifling hot words, and he was controlling a temper that almost slipped its bonds. Tim took a longer look and liked what he saw. She wasn't brooding anymore, that was obvious. If anything, she was seething.

"Will you call Cherry and tell her I'm putting lunch on the table, Todd?" Meg called from the kitchen.

"Sure."

He put the car away and went to find his daughter, who was riding in the fenced arena, going around the barrels very slowly.

"Hi, Dad," she called, waving her hand.

"How's it going?" he yelled.

"Fine! I'm working slowly, like Jane told me to. How is she?"

"She's all right," he replied. "Meg's got lunch ready. Put your horse up and come on in."

"Okay, Dad!"

He stuck his hands into the pockets of his slacks and went back to the house. Meg had coffee and sandwiches on the long dining-room table, where Jane and Tim were sitting. He washed up and then they waited for Cherry, who came to join them a few minutes later.

"You'll need some food before you start on those books again." Tim chuckled, watching Todd raid the sandwich platter before he passed it along to his daughter. She helped herself, talking animatedly to Meg and Tim.

"I love to see a man with a healthy appetite," Jane murmured, to needle him. She was sitting next to him and nibbling delicately on her own sandwich.

Todd glared at her. She finished her sandwich and leaned toward him, sniffing.

"Umm," she murmured huskily, so that only he could hear while Tim and Meg were talking. "What *is* that cologne you're wearing? It's very sexy."

He didn't reply, reaching for his coffee cup instead with an expression as hard as steel.

"Jane, Todd said that he thinks he can get us operating in the black," Tim said to Jane.

"Really?" Jane smiled at him. "Can we afford it?"

He sipped his coffee and put a sandwich on his plate. "It's going to require some belt tightening, if that's what you mean," he said, refusing to rise to the bait. He looked directly at her. "And you're going to have to borrow enough to make some improvements."

She let out a long breath. "I was afraid you'd say that. I don't think we can borrow any more."

"Yes, you can," he said, without telling her why he was sure of it. His name would convince any banker to let her have the loan, if he was willing to stand behind it. And he was. He dealt in amounts that would make her mind boggle. The amount she needed to get the ranch on its feet was paltry indeed compared to his annual budget. His backing would give her a good start, and it was an investment that would pay dividends one day. Not that he expected to capitalize on it. He'd be in the guise of a guardian angel, not a working partner.

She gnawed her lower lip, all signs of humor gone. "What would we have to do?"

He outlined the changes he had in mind, including the improvements to buildings, putting the stallions out to stud, building a breeding herd, leasing out un-used land and applying for land development funds through government agencies.

Jane caught her breath mentally at the picture he painted of what could become a successful ranch, with horses for its foundation instead of cattle. It had been her father's dream to make the ranch self-supporting. Jane had tried, but she had no real knowledge of fi-nance. All she knew was horses.

"Besides these changes," Todd added, "you have a name with commercial potential. It's a hell of a shame not to capitalize on it. Have you considered endorsing a line of Western clothing? Other rodeo stars have gone into such licensing. Why not you?"

"I . . . couldn't do that," she said hesitantly.

"Why?"

"I'm not going to be photographed in a wheel-chair!"

"You wouldn't have to be," he said curtly. "The wheelchair is only temporary. Didn't the doctor tell you so?"

She rubbed her temples. She was on the way to a king-size headache. Todd Burke headache number one, she thought whimsically, and had to bite back a grin.

"I can't think that anyone would be interested in a line of clothing advertised by a has-been."

"You aren't a has-been," Cherry said quietly. "You're a legend. My gosh, at the riding school I went to they had posters of you all over the place!"

She knew the poster had been made, but she didn't realize that anybody had actually paid money for one. She looked blankly at Cherry.

"You've forgotten, haven't you?" Tim asked. "I told you that they had to reprint the posters because of the demand. But it was right after the wreck. I guess you weren't listening."

"No," she agreed. "I was in shock." She looked at Todd. "If there's a chance that we can make the ranch into a paying operation, I want to take it. If I lose, okay. But I'm not going under without a fight. Do whatever you like about the loan and the financing, and then just point me in the right direction. I'll do whatever you want me to."

"All right," Todd said. "We'll give it a shot."

Four

Todd insisted on going to the Jacobsville bank alone when he went to apply for the loan. It wouldn't do for Jane to find out how he was going to manage financing for his improvement program.

The bank manager was sworn to silence and he had received Todd's written backing for the loan. A few phone calls and it was all arranged. He had the necessary amount credited to Jane's account and then he set about replacing old equipment and hiring contractors to make improvements to existing buildings on the ranch.

When Jane saw the first bill, she almost called for a shot of whiskey.

"I can't afford this," she gasped.

"Yes, you can," Todd assured her. He sat across from her at the desk in the study. "You certainly can't afford to let things go further downhill. In the long run, maintenance is much less expensive than replacing everything you own."

She groaned. "But the electric fence . . . !"

"Less expensive than replacing a wood and barbed wire one, and less damaging to livestock," he said. "I've also contacted the Soil Conservation Service about assistance with a pond for water impoundment."

"A tank," she said absently. "We call them tanks here in Texas."

He raised an eyebrow but he made no further comment. "Another thing," he added, "I've arranged for some roof repairs on the house. You've got pots and pans all over the place to catch the water from leaks. If you don't fix the roof, you'll have to replace it. The wood will eventually rot."

"How will I pay for it all?" she asked the ceiling.

"I'm glad you asked," he said with a smile. He leaned back, propping one big booted foot against the lower rung of a nearby chair. In the pose, he looked lean and fit and very masculine. Jane had to control a sigh, and hide the surge of attraction she felt.

"Well?" she prompted.

"I'm advertising two of the stallions for stud purposes," he said. "They're champions with well-known bloodlines and they'll command a high price. I'm also going to purchase two or three good brood mares. We're going to breed them to other champions. Their offspring will add to our own blood stock, and the ones we don't add to the stud, we'll sell.''

"We'll need a better barn," she began.

"We're going to build one," he said. "I've already hired a contractor."

"You take my breath away," she said, leaning back. "But all this will take time, and the ranch is on the edge of bankruptcy as it is," she added worriedly.

"That's where you come in," he said quietly. "I've approached a clothing manufacturer in Houston. They're interested in having you promote a line of women's Western wear, primarily leisure wear, such as jeans."

"Do they know...?"

He nodded. "They won't photograph you in a wheelchair." He told her the sum they were offering and she flushed.

"You're kidding!" she bellowed.

He shook his head. "Not at all. You'll want to see the manufacturer, of course. I wouldn't expect you to endorse clothing you haven't seen."

She was excited at the prospect of having her name on a line of clothes, but she was afraid to become overenthusiastic. No deal was final until contracts were signed. And there might be a reason to keep her from signing. "I won't endorse something cheap or sloppy," she agreed.

"I'm fairly sure that this is a reputable clothier," he told her, "and not a fly-by-night enterprise. We'll see. They'd like to come down and talk to you next Friday."

She smiled. "Okay."

He watched her with interest. Her face was animated, her blue eyes twinkling. She looked like a different woman. Her hair was in its usual long braid, held in place with a rubber band, a few wisps of it escaping down into her face. She brushed it away impatiently and his eyes fell reluctantly to the soft thrust of her breasts against the knit fabric of her blue pullover shirt.

"Stop that," she said at once, lifting her chin. "If I can't ogle you, you can't ogle me."

His eyebrows arched. "I don't remember saying you couldn't ogle me."

"Yes, you did. Quite emphatically. This is a business relationship now. Let's keep it that way."

He chuckled softly, then pursed his lips. "Are you sure you want to?" he asked with a honeyed drawl.

She was already out of her league, and she knew it, but she wasn't going to let *him* gain the upper hand. She simply smiled. "Yes, I'm sure," she told him. "Now what time next Friday do these people want to see me?"

By the next Thursday morning, all the arrangements were finalized for the meeting with the clothing manufacturers and the public relations people. The improvements on the house were underway, and noise had become a part of everyday life.

Jane escaped to the corral with Cherry after breakfast to get away from the carpenters. Todd was holed up in the study with the telephone, and the door was firmly closed. Jane wondered how he could hear above the chaos.

"Noise, noise," she groaned, holding her head. "I'm going to shoot those men just to get the hammers stopped!"

"It will be better to get the leaks stopped," Cherry told her with a cheeky grin.

"Ha!"

Cherry finished saddling the nice little quarter horse mare her father had bought her. "I named her Feather. Isn't she pretty?" she asked.

"She's very pretty, and she can do those turns blindfolded," Jane assured her. "You have to trust her, Cherry. You have to sit loose in the saddle and not pull on the reins. If you can do that, she'll make those turns as tight as a drum."

Cherry slumped a little. "I can't," she said miserably. She sat down on a bale of hay beside Jane, holding the reins in one hand while Feather nibbled at the hay. "I do try, Jane, but when she goes so fast around those turns..."

"You're afraid you'll fall off," Jane finished for her.

"Well, there's that, too," Cherry said. She picked at a piece of straw and snapped it between her fingers. "But it's the horse I'm most afraid for. My first time on the barrel-racing circuit, a rider went down and so did the horse. The fall broke the horse's leg." She threw away the straw. "They were going to put her down, but I begged and begged, and Dad bought her for me. She lives with a relative back in Wyoming, and she's doing fine, but I've had a hard time racing ever since that day."

Todd hadn't told Jane that. She slid an affectionate arm around the girl and hugged her warmly.

"That's very rare, you know," she said gently.
"People in rodeo, people who ride, love their horses.
Nobody ever uses an animal in a way that will harm
it—not if they want to stay in rodeo. Cherry, I've been
riding for twenty years, since I was five, and I've never
had a horse go down under me when I was barrel racing. Never. I've fallen off," she added humorously.
"And once I had a rib broken when a horse kicked as
I fell. But when I was racing, there wasn't a single
mishap."

"Really?" Cherry asked, brightening.

"Really. Riding skill is largely a matter of having a
well-trained horse and then not trying to exert too
much control over the horse. Haven't you watched
riders put quarter horses through their paces?"

"Sure. They're wonderful to watch. All a good rider
has to do is just sit and the horse does all the work of
cutting a steer out of a herd."

"That's right. The horse knows his job, and does it.
Where the problem begins is when the rider thinks he
knows more than the horse and tries to take control."

Cherry's gray eyes widened. "Oh. Oh!"

Jane grinned. "You're getting the picture, aren't
you?"

"Wow! Am I ever!"

"Now let that sink in while you're putting Feather
through her paces," she suggested. "And don't rush.
Just go slow and easy."

"Slow and easy," Cherry echoed.

"What is this, a conference?" Todd asked from the doorway.

"Cowgirl talk." His daughter chuckled. "Hi, Dad! Want to come and watch me?"

"Sure, in just a minute. I have to talk to the boss."

"I always thought *you* were the boss," she murmured as she went past, sharing a private joke with him.

He chuckled. "So did I," he agreed.

"See you later, Jane!" Cherry called. She led Feather out into the sunlight and climbed aboard with ease.

"She looks happy," Todd remarked.

He was looking very Western in his jeans and boots and blue patterned shirt with the gray Stetson pulled low over his eyes. He had a rodeo rider's physique, square shouldered and lean hipped, with long, powerful legs. Jane tried not to notice and failed miserably. It was a good thing there was so much shadow in the barn.

"We were talking about barrel racing. She told me about the injured horse you bought for her, back in Wyoming. That was kind of you."

"Kind." He shrugged. "I didn't stand a chance once she started crying. Tears wear me down."

"I'll have to remember that."

He cocked an eyebrow. "*Cherry's* tears," he said emphatically. "I'm immune to any others."

She snapped her fingers. "Darn the luck!"

His pale eyes swept over her slender body. She hadn't come down here in the wheelchair. She had her crutches instead. "That's dangerous," he said pointedly. "You could take a bad fall trying to maneuver through the gravel."

"No pain, no gain," she told him. "I can manage or I wouldn't have tried. I don't enjoy spending weeks in bed."

He decided that it might be best to ignore the remark. "I've been talking to Cherry's mother. She does want her this weekend after all," he said. "She's going to take Cherry shopping, so I'll drive her up about ten tomorrow morning. With any luck, I'll be back before those clothing representatives arrive. But in any case you need to have your attorney read the contract before you sign it."

"I know that," she said.

"Good."

She got up from the bale slowly and held on to her crutches, easing them under her arms. It was hard going, balancing on them, but she was doing better at it every day.

"Do Cherry and her mother get along?" she asked as they left the barn and went toward the corral where Cherry was practicing.

"Yes, most of the time. Cherry doesn't like her stepfather."

"I don't imagine she does. Many children of divorced parents live with a hope that their real parents will get together again, or so I've heard."

"Cherry knows better. She hated the way it was before the divorce. Too many arguments can make home life hell for a young girl."

"I suppose so."

"Didn't your parents ever argue?" he asked her.

"I don't know. My mother died when I was barely old enough to start school. My dad raised me. Well, my dad and Tim and Meg," Jane amended.

"It must have hit you hard to lose him."

She nodded. "At least I still had Tim and Meg. That made it easier. In an odd way, the injury helped, too. It gave me a challenge, kept me going. If I'd had time to sit and brood, I think I might have gone crazy. I miss him so."

Her voice was husky with feeling. He glanced down at her with mingled emotions. "I lost my mother nine years ago," he said. "My dad followed her two years later. I remember how it felt. We were a close-knit family."

"I'm sorry."

His broad shoulders rose and fell. "People die. It's the way of things."

"That doesn't make it easy."

"No."

They stopped at the corral fence. Cherry was leaning over Feather's neck, talking softly to her. She glanced at Todd and Jane, grinned and suddenly urged Feather into a gallop.

As they watched, she bent low over Feather's mane, her hands not clinging to the reins, closed her eyes and let nature take its course. Feather took the first barrel so low that she seemed to slither around it, easily regaining her balance and heading for the barrel at the other end of the corral at the same feverish pace. She circled that one with the same ease, and kept going until an elated Cherry whooped loudly and gently reined her in on the side of the corral where the surprised, delighted adults were standing.

"Did you see?" Cherry burst out, red-faced and laughing so hard that tears ran down her dusty cheeks. "Oh, did you see! I did it!"

"I saw," Jane said with a smile. "Cherry, you're just great!"

"You're the great one," the girl said shyly. "After all, you told me how to do it. I won't be afraid anymore. Feather knows just what to do. All I have to do is let her."

"That's right. Slow and easy. You're doing fine now."

"I am, aren't I?" Cherry asked.

"You're a champ," Todd said as he found his voice, his eyes sparkling with pleasure. "I'm proud of you."

"Thanks, Dad!" She laughed again, and gave Feather her head.

"Don't overdo!" he yelled after her.

"No way!" came floating back over the sound of hoofbeats.

"So much for slow and easy," Jane murmured, watching the young girl.

Todd had a booted foot propped on the lowest fence rail. He glanced down at Jane with hooded eyes, unsmiling. She looked frail, but her slender body had a nice curve to it, and her breasts were firm and pert under that open-neck knit shirt. Her hair was loose around her shoulders for a change, faintly wavy and very pretty. Like Jane herself.

"Slow and easy," he said half under his breath, thinking of another exercise, one that made his heart begin to race.

Jane heard the deep note in his voice and looked up. Her eyes were trapped in the gray glitter under his hat brim. His lean hand came up to her face, cupping her cheek in its warmth while his thumb slowly traced the line of her upper lip until he made it tremble.

She couldn't get a breath of air into her starving lungs. She swallowed, and her lips parted helplessly while she struggled to find a teasing remark to break the tension.

Todd's own lips opened as he watched hers. His thumb slid down to the edge of her white teeth and caressed it lazily. Her mouth was as soft as a petal, warm, full.

Then suddenly, somehow, she was closer to him. She could see the pulse in his neck throbbing, feel the heat off his body. That cologne he wore was in her nostrils as the wind picked up and blew at his back.

He hadn't moved. His body was open and she was at an angle to that propped leg, so that they were standing in an intimacy that was respectable and tantalizing at the same time. She could almost feel the hard pressure of his legs against hers, the threat of his body so close to hers. Her heart was beating madly in her throat. Her eyes fell to his hard mouth, where it parted, and for an endless space of seconds, she saw it in her mind's eye, pressed ruthlessly, demandingly, against her own.

His breath was warm and unsteady. She could taste the coffee on it. He breathed and she felt his breath against her parted lips where his thumb was exploring. She felt it, felt him, felt the hunger that had been a stranger all her life until now.

She moved closer, as if he willed her to, moved jerkily on her crutches until she was standing right in the fork of his body and she could feel him just barely touching her—his long legs, his chest, his flat stomach, his hips—barely, barely touching, teasing, intimidating.

She made a husky, whimpering little sound in her throat and suddenly pressed herself to him.

Tim whistled loudly, Feather snorted, the roar of a car's engine all exploded into the tension and Jane actually moaned.

She jerked away from Todd so fast that she fell against the fence. His arm shot out to spare her the impact of a fall, righting her and the crutches, all without looking directly into her eyes. He was as shaken as she seemed to be, and angry that she'd gotten to him at all.

"Damn you." He bit off the words furiously.

She hit his broad chest with a flat hand. "You started that!" she accused hotly. "Damn you, too!"

"Todd! That building contractor's coming up the driveway!" Tim called before he went back to meet the man.

"I told you," Todd continued, ignoring the interruption, "that I'm not in the mood for an affair!"

"I'm the one on crutches," she snapped back. "It isn't as if I threw myself at you!"

"Isn't it? I didn't come to you!"

"Todd!" Tim called again.

He released Jane from his furious glare long enough to look toward Tim. "I'll be right there!"

Tim made a thumbs-up gesture and greeted the newcomer.

Todd looked back at Jane, who was pale but not backing down an inch. Her chin was thrust out and she was looking at him with eyes as angry as his own.

"You know what you do to a man with those bedroom eyes," he accused curtly. "You've probably had more lovers than I have."

"And just think, *I* didn't have to *pay* them!"

His breath inverted and he seemed to grow taller and more threatening in the space of a few seconds. "You . . . !" he began in a thunderous undertone.

She pulled herself up as tall as she could with the crutches and her hand slipped, grabbing at the crosspiece for support. She managed it, barely.

The pathetic little movement brought Todd back to his senses. Disabled she might be, but she had spirit. She wouldn't back down, or give up, no matter how formidable the opposition. He was furious, but even through his anger he felt admiration for her spunk.

"When you get back on your feet properly," he said deeply, "we'll have this out."

"What's the matter, big man, afraid to try your boxing gloves on a woman with crutches?" she taunted.

He chuckled despite his bad temper. "Not when the woman's got a switchblade in her tongue," he retorted. "Hellcat!"

"Pig!"

His eyebrows lifted. "Who, me?"

"Oink, oink!"

He searched her flushed face, her tousled hair, her wide angry blue eyes for a long moment, aware of faint regret. He wasn't going to let himself be seduced into another dead-end relationship. But, oh, he was tempted. This woman wasn't like anyone he'd ever known.

"And don't drool over me," she snapped.

"Optimist," he countered lazily.

She made a rough sound under her breath and turned unsteadily on her crutches. "I want to be there when you talk to the contractor. It's my ranch he'll be working on."

"I planned for you to meet him," he assured her. "That's why he's here."

"You might have given me a little advance notice," she said angrily.

"That's why I came down to the barn in the first place," he told her. "We got sidetracked."

"*You* got sidetracked," she accused with a harsh glare. "You started it."

"I had help," he returned. He stared her down. "How many men did it take to perfect that simpering, hungry look of yours?"

She glared and turned away. She didn't answer him, hobbling along on her crutches as fast as she could.

"If I could balance on one leg, I'd crack one of these crutches over your head," she said icily.

"You must have given the good doctor fits," he mused. "He still drools over you."

"He's a good man," she said shortly. "And he knows me."

"I don't doubt it," he drawled meaningfully.

She flushed. The going was rough on that gravel. She blew a strand of hair out of her face as she soldiered on.

The contractor was leaning against the hood of a nice green Mercedes, waiting for them. He was lean and elegant looking, darkly tanned, with black eyes in a swarthy face topped by straight, long black hair in a ponytail.

"This is Sloan Hayes," Todd introduced them. The Native American builder shook hands with Jane and then with Tim.

"We haven't met, but I've certainly heard of you," Jane said with a polite smile. Most people had. He was very famous and she was surprised that Todd knew him. "This is a small job . . ."

"We're glad to get it," Hayes replied suavely. "It's been slow lately," he hedged. "Your, uh, manager here has gone over the plans with me, but he wanted you to see them before we finalize the work. I brought the blueprints along so that you could inspect them."

"That's very nice of you," Jane said with a smile.

He cocked an eyebrow and smiled back. "I should have mentioned that I've been a rodeo fan all my life. I've seen you ride." He shook his head. "Hell of a shame about the accident. I'm sorry."

She was surprised, but not offended, by his openness. "I'm sorry, too, but life has these pitfalls. We have to adapt."

"Any idea what you'll substitute for rodeo in your life?" he continued.

She smiled. "How about raising champion horses?"

He chuckled. "Sounds like a winner. That's one of my own hobbies." His eyes narrowed appreciatively on her slender body.

Todd's face went stiff. "The plans?" he prompted.

Sloan gave him a deep look. "I'll get them."

"We can look them over in the study," Jane said. "Tim, will you have Meg get some coffee and cake and bring it on a tray when she's ready?"

"Sure thing!" Tim said, grinning.

Jane smiled at Todd as they waited for Sloan Hayes to get his blueprints. "He's very nice," she said with a deliberate sweetness. "I think this project is going to be a lot of fun."

"Just don't get too wound up in the project director," he cautioned. "He isn't marriage material, but he likes women...."

"Is *that* why you hired him? Thanks!" she said under her breath and smiled broadly when Sloan joined them on the porch.

"Here, let me help you with those crutches," the builder offered as they went into the house.

"Why, how very kind of you!" Jane said enthusiastically.

Todd followed them inside, the gnashing of his teeth all but audible. Complications were breaking out all over. First the redheaded doctor, now the builder. Well, he wasn't joining any queues and he didn't want her in the first place. Having settled that in the privacy of his own mind, he forced himself to concentrate on the business at hand.

They went over the blueprints. Jane had several questions, but all in all, she was very satisfied with what the builder had drawn up.

"Do we need so much space in the barn?" she asked finally, when they were drinking coffee and eating slices of Meg's wonderful lemon pound cake.

"You do if you're serious about turning this place into a stud ranch," Sloan said quietly. "You have to have immaculate facilities for the livestock. That sort of thing doesn't go unnoticed by customers. There will be a certain amount of socializing necessary, also. And you'll have to do some renovation to the house to make it fit in with the overall look of the ranch."

She bit her lower lip and glanced at Todd worriedly.

"You can do it," he said simply. "The money's there. It's all arranged."

"I didn't think that far ahead," she said, troubled.

"You'll have to," Sloan said. "This change is going to foster others. It's a commitment."

She stared down into her lap. She wasn't sure she wanted such a change.

"We'll talk about it later," Todd said. "Meanwhile, sleep on it before you decide. Sloan's got a few other jobs to finish first."

"That's right," the builder said with a nice smile. "You don't have to jump into anything. Weigh the consequences. Then decide what you want to do."

"I will. Thank you for being patient," she said gently.

He smiled at her. "Oh, I'm known for my patience," he said, tongue-in-cheek. "Ask Todd."

Todd lifted an eyebrow. "I won't lie for you."

"I would for you," the other man said with hidden intent. "In fact, I have." Which was true, because Sloan had put up a warehouse for Todd's computer company, and now he was keeping mum about Todd's real background.

"Have some more coffee and shut up," Todd murmured with a grin.

"Point taken. Now about these outbuildings," he told Jane. "This is what I'd suggest . . ."

By the time he left, Jane had a picture of what the ranch would look like once it had been transformed. The cost was enormous, but the profit could be enormous as well.

Now, it all rested on her ability to sell her name for that endorsement, so that she could afford the improvements. But she wasn't going to say yes unless she felt she was doing the right thing. And she wouldn't know that until she met the manufacturer. She was going to reserve judgment until the next day, when they conferred.

Five

Jane barely slept that night, wondering what would come of her meeting with the clothier and the company's public relations representative. It didn't help that Todd left early the next morning with Cherry for Victoria.

"I'll be back before they get here," he assured Jane. "Stop brooding."

"I'll try. It's a big decision. I just hope that they'll ask me to endorse a line I can feel comfortable putting my name on." She hugged Cherry, and the girl returned the embrace with genuine fondness. In a short time, they'd become close. "Have a good time with your mother, and have fun shopping."

"Sure. You take care of yourself. No dancing," she teased, nodding toward the crutches.

Jane laughed softly. "Okay."

"I'll see you Monday."

Jane nodded, and waved them off. Todd looked glad to go. Perhaps, like her, he needed some breathing space. She wondered if he planned to spend the weekend at the ranch or go off on his own. Probably, she thought bitterly, he had plenty of women just waiting for the chance to go out with him. As good-looking as he was, she didn't doubt his attraction for the opposite sex. In a way, she was glad that she was exempt from his attentions. The very brief glimpse she'd had of his ardor the day before at the corral made her knees weak in retrospect. He wasn't the sort of man to play games with inexperienced women. He didn't know that she was inexperienced, either, and she had no intention of giving herself away.

She went back inside, glad of the time she was getting to distance herself from Todd's disturbing presence. She went over the books, amazed at what he'd accomplished in so short a time. He really was a wizard with figures. How, she wondered, could a man with such superb business sense spend his life working for someone else? He could have made a fortune by putting his analytical mind to work in his own interests. Perhaps he had no ambition, she decided finally.

She might have changed her mind if she could have seen him later that morning, sitting behind the desk in the president's office at Burke-Hathaway Business Systems. He'd long since bought out the Hathaway who was the old head of the company, but he left the name. It was known in south Texas, as Burke wasn't, and that made it good for business.

He made several pressing telephone calls, dictated letters and made arrangements to have leftover business sent down by fax. He'd installed a machine in the study, and he told his secretary that he'd telephone her with instructions as to when he wanted business documents sent. It wouldn't do for Jane to be in the study when he was working. He felt a twinge of guilt at keeping this from her, but after all, he *had* told her that he would be keeping his job and working for her on the side. In effect, he was.

That might bother him one day, but there was no reason for her to know the truth about his private life. She was just a temporarily disabled woman whom he felt sorry for. On a whim he'd decided to help her. It was a diversion, a challenge. Life had gone sour for him lately, with his business prospering and orders coming in faster than he could fill them. He'd been stagnating with nothing to challenge his quick mind. He had good people, subordinates, who did all the really interesting work—inventing new software, balancing books, marketing. All he did was public relations work, making contacts, conducting high-level meetings, signing contracts and talking to bankers and stockholders. The thing that had made the company fun in the first place was the risk. He'd left any real risk behind when the company became one of the Fortune 500. These days, he was the chief executive officer and president of Burke-Hathaway.

He was a figurehead.

But not on the Parker ranch. No, sir. There, he was necessary. He was the one thing standing between Jane and bankruptcy, and it made him feel good to know that he could make such a difference in her life. There was the challenge he needed to put the color back into his life. And it was helping Cherry, too. She and Jane were already friends. The girl hadn't had much fun in her life, but she really loved rodeo and Jane was the perfect person to help her learn the ropes. In fact, it had helped Jane already. She was less broody and more determined than ever to get her broken body back into some semblance of normalcy. All around, to sign on as Jane's business manager was one of the better decisions of Todd's life.

Then if it was such a great move, why, he asked himself as he signed letters on the mahogany desk, did he feel so morose and out of humor? He and Jane should have been friends, but they weren't. Jane fought him at every turn, and all at once, yesterday, he'd precipitated a physical awareness in her that he regretted. She was vulnerable now, and he should have known better than to start something he couldn't finish.

She was so lovely, he thought angrily. Under different circumstances, he'd have made a dead set at her. But although she was old enough to have had lovers, he wondered about that side of her life. The doctor was interested in her, but there was no hint of real intimacy between the two of them. Old lovers would show it. They couldn't help but show it.

"Mr. Burke, you have to initial this contract as well," his secretary reminded him gently, pointing to two circles in the margin.

"Sorry." He initialed all three copies in the appropriate places and pushed them toward her. "Anything else pressing?"

"No, sir, not until next week."

He got up from the desk. "I'll be in and out," he said. "Mostly out. But I've left a number where I can be reached in case of an emergency." His steely gray eyes met hers. "Notice that I said *emergency*."

"Yes, sir." Miss Emory was in her early fifties and unflappable. She smiled. "Are you in disguise, sir?"

He chuckled. "In a manner of speaking, yes, so take care."

"Yes, sir."

"I'll check with you periodically. If anything urgent crops up, fax me. You don't need to explain anything, just state that I need to phone you. Sign your first name, not your last, to the fax. That way if anyone sees it, they'll just think I'm getting messages from a girlfriend."

Miss Emory chuckled. "Yes, sir."

He stacked the paperwork on the edge of the desk and left Miss Emory to deal with it. He had a feeling that she was going to earn more than her regular check for the next few weeks. He hoped he wasn't going to regret the decision that had taken him to Jacobsville.

The executive vice president from SlimTogs leisure wear was a young woman named Micki Lane. She had a nice smile and a firm handshake. Jane liked her at once. Her companion, however, was another sort altogether. Rick Wardell was a high-powered promoter with a fixed smile and determination in every line of his body. He verbally pushed Micki to one side and began to outline what would be expected of Jane if the company decided to use her.

Micki started to protest, but she was no match for Rick's verbal onslaught. Jane, however, was.

She held up a firm hand when the man was in full spate. "Wait a minute," she said pleasantly. "I haven't said that I want or need to do this endorsement. Furthermore, I'm not endorsing anything that I haven't seen."

"But we're very well-known," Rick said, sounding less confident than before.

"Of course you're well-known to most people," Jane replied. "But not to me," she said emphatically. "I'm rodeo from the boots up. I come from a long line of rodeo people. That means that if I endorse a product, a lot of fans will buy it. I want to be sure that I'm putting my name on something that's attractive, fairly priced and durable."

Rick's face tautened. "Listen, honey, you don't seem to understand that we're doing you a favor—" he began angrily.

"Nobody calls me *honey* unless I say they can," Jane interrupted. "I'm no wallpaper girl." Jane's blue eyes were flashing like lightning, and the man's mouth closed abruptly as he realized that he'd overstepped the mark and the situation was deteriorating rapidly.

Before Jane could say anything more, the borrowed car Todd was driving pulled up behind Rick's flashy little red sports car. He got out and joined the small group, taking in the situation with one long look.

"Burke! Glad you're here. I don't think Miss Parker understands what a favor we'd be doing her to put her name on this new line," Rick began, smiling as if he were certain that another man would surely side with him. "Maybe you can talk some sense into her."

"Surely the 'favor' extends in both directions?" Todd interrupted suavely. "Or hasn't your sales manager told you that several boutiques are queueing up already to place orders for any merchandise endorsed by Jane Parker?"

Rick laughed nervously. "Well, certainly, but..." He laughed again. "Perhaps we could start over?"

Micki was standing near Jane, looking irritated.

"Ms. Lane, isn't it?" Todd asked, and moved forward to shake hands with her. His eyes narrowed. "Excuse me, but I thought you were sent here to negotiate with Miss Parker?" He glanced pointedly toward Rick Wardell as he spoke.

"I was," Micki replied. "Mr. Wardell is in charge of sales and promotion."

Jane smiled at Rick. It wasn't a nice smile. She hadn't liked his condescending tone. "In order to have something to promote, I have to sign a contract. Frankly I don't think there's a chance in hell that it's going to happen. But it was nice of you to come out, Mr. Wardell. You, too, Miss Lane."

Micki stepped in front of Rick. "I'd like to show you our new line of jeans," she said quietly, "along with some of the new T-shirts we've adapted to imitate rodeo styling—with fringe and sequins and beads. They're machine-washable and guaranteed not to shrink or fade. I think you might like them."

Jane was impressed. She smiled. "Well..."

Micki glanced toward a very defensive-looking Rick, and the buried steel in her makeup began to show itself in her cool smile. "Mr. Wardell wanted to come along so that he could meet you. Now that he has, I'm sure that he won't mind leaving the contractual discussion in my hands. Will you, Mr. Wardell?" she added pointedly.

He smiled uncertainly, then cleared his throat. "As you say, that might be best." He grinned, showing all his teeth. "Nice to have met you, Miss Parker, and I hope we'll be doing business. Burke." He nodded, still grinning, and turned to stride quickly back toward his sports car.

"If I sign anything, it had better have a clause that that man isn't to come within shooting range of me," Jane said bluntly, glaring after him. "I hate being talked down to!"

"Rick has his drawbacks, but he could sell ice to Eskimos. We're slowly drawing him into the twentieth century," Micki said with a grin. "I'll have a few words with the division boss about it when I get back. Meanwhile, couldn't I show you these samples, now that I'm here?"

"Well...I guess so," Jane agreed.

Micki smiled and went to get the case from her own car, a neat little tan sedan.

"It seems as though I arrived in the nick of time," Todd said quietly.

Jane looked up at him, still defensive. "Just in time to save that man's life, for a fact. The condescending, stuck-up son of a—"

"He's a super salesman," he said pointedly. "He's a master at sucking up to people when he feels he has to."

"He'll think he's found lemon heaven if he tries it on me!"

Todd chuckled. He liked the way she looked when she was animated. "You've got a temper."

"No kidding!"

"Calm down," he advised. "I won't try to force you to sign with them, but it would be to your advantage. The money for these repairs has to come from somewhere. This would almost pay for it. And if the line is as good as Micki says it is, you won't have a reason to refuse."

"I can give you a good one, and it drives a red sports car!"

"You won't even have to talk to him again. I promise."

She eased up a little. "Well, if you promise."

"That's the spirit."

Micki came back, the sun shining on her sleek black hair. She was a pretty woman, slight and sedate looking, with dark eyes and an olive complexion. She smiled, and her eyes sparkled.

"Can we sit down?" she asked. "I've been on my feet all day and I'm tired."

Probably, Jane thought sagely, because the woman could see that Jane was tiring as she leaned heavily on the crutches. Business sense and diplomacy were a nice mixture, and Jane knew even before she saw and approved of the clothing samples that she was going to sign that contract.

She gave the contract to her attorney to look over, but she sent Micki off with her assurances that she would do the endorsement. Micki was relieved and elated when she shook hands with both of them and left. Todd watched her out the door, his lips pursed thoughtfully.

"She isn't married," Jane remarked, aware of a faint twinge of jealousy that she was going to smother at once. "And she's very pretty."

He turned, his hands deep in the pockets of his tan slacks. Muscles rippled in his long arms, emphasized by the clinging knit of his yellow sports shirt. "So she is," he agreed. "But she's off limits."

"Why?"

"I don't seduce business contacts," he said frankly. "It's bad for my image."

Her eyebrows lifted. "I didn't know accountants worried about things like that."

Business executives did. But he couldn't say it. He'd almost made a serious blunder. He laughed off his own remark. "I might work for her one day," he explained. "It's better if I don't get involved with potential bosses."

"Or current ones?" She was fishing and grinning. "Thank God!"

He glowered at her. "There's no need to look so relieved."

"Sorry. It slipped out. Erase it from your memory." She leaned back on the sofa and stifled a yawn. "It's been a long day. I'm sleepy."

"Why don't you stretch out there and take a nap?" he asked. "I've got some figures to catch up and Meg and Tim have gone grocery shopping. You've got nothing to do, have you?"

"Not right now, anyway." She stretched back onto the cushions, stifling a grimace. She was sore from the walking she'd done for the past two days on the crutches. "I suppose I'm a little less fit than I thought," she said with a self-conscious smile. She tucked a pillow under her head. "The crutches are hard going." Her eyes closed. "But I hate the wheelchair."

"Go to sleep," he said gruffly. He stood there watching her, his eyes narrow on her pale face in its frame of long, silky blond hair. She did look like a fashion doll, all the way up and down, from her pretty face to her slender, curvaceous body and long, elegant legs. He liked the way she looked. But he couldn't afford to pay too much attention to it. This was a very temporary job, and soon he was going to be back in the fast lane. He had to be objective and remote.

He turned and went into the study, closing the door gently. He had enough paperwork of his own to occupy him until supper, much less the additional burden of Jane's. It was a shame that things in his company had become complicated at just the wrong time. But he'd manage. The challenge was refreshing. He couldn't remember when he'd enjoyed himself so much.

* * *

In the weeks that followed, a bond developed between Jane and Cherry. They were all but inseparable, especially out at the corral where Cherry worked on perfecting her technique on horseback. She was better. She had self-confidence and the turns weren't making her hesitate. She gave Feather her head and watched the little mare incredulously as she sailed through her paces.

Jane was proud of her pupil, and that showed, too. She spent less time brooding about her slow progress and began to show marked improvement as her therapy sessions became fewer and farther between.

Todd, on the other hand, was finding his job harder by the day. The paperwork and the building work were easy, but being close to Jane all the time was wearing him down. An accidental touch of their fingers sent his heart racing. A look that lingered too long made him tingle down to his toes. He found himself watching her for no reason at all, except that he liked to look at her. And his vulnerability made him bad-tempered. He was spending a lot of time with Micki Lane, going over the contracts with the attorneys before Jane signed them. She was pretty and interested in him, and he needed a diversion. So without counting the cost, he called her up and invited her to a dance.

The dance at the Jacobsville Civic Center was one of the monthly events that passed for socializing in Jacobsville. Jane had gone to them frequently before her accident, often with Copper Coltrain. But she'd given up dancing because of her injury. When Cherry mentioned casually that her dad was taking that pretty leisure wear executive to it, Jane was unprepared for the surge of jealousy she felt. She liked Micki, but it was hard to think of her with Todd. At least, she thought miserably, she'd have Cherry for company.

Only it didn't work out that way. Cherry accepted a last-minute invitation to spend the weekend with her mother and caught an early bus to Victoria. Then Tim and Meg announced that they'd be gone, too. Jane felt miserable and tried desperately not to show it. It seemed that everyone was going to desert her.

Todd thought that Jane seemed pale when he was ready to leave to pick Micki up that evening. He paused with the car keys jingling in his pocket. "You don't mind being here alone?" he asked. He looked very attractive in tan slacks, cream-colored boots and a patterned Western shirt and black string tie.

"Of course not," Jane said proudly. "I'm used to being by myself when Tim and Meg go to visit their daughter. They go at least one Saturday a month and they don't get in until late," she added.

He looked concerned. He didn't like having her on her own so far from any neighbors.

"This isn't a big city," she said, exasperated. "For heaven's sake, nobody's going to break in and kill me! I've got a shotgun over there behind the door, and I know how to use it!"

"If you have time to load it," he muttered. "Do you know where the shells are?"

She made a face. "I can find them if I have to."

He threw up his hands. "Oh, that's very reassuring! I hope any potential intruders are polite enough to wait while you do that!"

"I'm almost twenty-six years old!" she raged at him. "I can take care of myself without any tall, blond nursemaids! You just go on and mind your own business. I'm looking forward to a quiet evening with a good book!"

"I can see how that will benefit you," he said sarcastically. He picked up the book on the table beside the end of the sofa where she was lounging in jeans and a loose green shirt. "A source book on the battle of the Alamo. How enlightening."

"I like to read history," she said.

"Romance novels might do you more good," he returned. "A little vicarious pleasure would be better than nothing, surely."

Her blue eyes flashed. "If I want romance, I know where to go looking for it!"

"I'm flattered," he said, deliberately provocative.

"Not *you*," she said angrily. "Never you! That's wishful thinking on your part. You're not that attractive to me!"

"Really?" He bent toward her. She averted her face, but he reached behind her head with a steely hand and turned her face up to his. She had one quick glimpse of flint-hard gray eyes before his hard mouth came down on hers.

She reached up instinctively to push at him, but his teeth were nibbling her shocked, set lips apart. He tasted of mint and smelled of sexy cologne. The clean scents seduced her as much as the sharp, teasing movements of his mouth.

Her fingers clenched on his shirtfront in token protest. She made a sound, but his free hand came to her throat and he began to smooth it in gentle caresses. She felt her breath catch as the lazy pressure of his mouth touched something hidden and secret, deep inside her body. She felt like a coiled spring that was suddenly loosened. Her quick intake of breath was echoed by the faint groan that pushed past his hard mouth into her parting lips.

He caught her grasping fingers and spread them against the front of his soft shirt, moving them sensually from side to side over the hard, warm muscles. His breathing quickened, as did hers, and his hand moved to press her mouth closer into the demanding contact with his.

Her faint whimper excited him. He gave in to the red-hot waves of pleasure, hardly aware that he'd moved until he felt her body under his as he eased down on the sofa with her.

She felt the cushions at her back, his lean strength touching her from shoulders to thigh, his arms around her, his mouth touching and lifting, seducing, demanding in a silence so fraught with emotion that she could hear the sound of her own heartbeat.

His hands were under her blouse, against the skin of her back, exploring her as if she belonged to him. One long leg was insinuating itself between both of hers, gently so as not to jar her, seductively slow.

She managed to get a fraction of an inch between her mouth and his, and she struggled for breath and presence of mind.

"No..." she whispered jerkily.

His left hand tangled in her long hair while the right one roughly unsnapped the pearly studs of his shirt. He was wearing nothing underneath the fabric, and without hesitation, he gently pushed her face against thick hair and clean, cologne-scented bare skin, coaxing her mouth to touch him just below his collarbone.

She hadn't experienced that sort of intimacy. She fought it, trying to remember that he was on his way to another woman.

He shifted, so that her lips were touching the hard, tight thrust of a male nipple. His hand, behind her head, guided her, insisted, without a single word.

She was curious and attracted, so she did what he wanted her to do. She wasn't prepared for the ripple of muscle under her mouth or the soft, tortured moan that sounded above her head.

She hesitated, but his hand contracted in her hair and he moaned again, shifting. She gave in, suckling him, tasting him in a heated interlude that made her lower body seem to swell with new sensations.

Both his hands were in her hair now, guiding her mouth around the fascinating territory of his chest. It expanded violently as she kissed him, and he groaned even as he laughed at the delight her touch gave him.

He moved to lie on his back, his mouth swollen, his eyes glittering with emotion, his chest bare and throbbing when she finally lifted her head to look down at him.

He smiled with a kind of secret fever, stretching so that the shirt fell away. He arched, holding her eyes.

She pressed both hands to the wall of his broad chest, testing the wiry silkiness of the hair that covered him, watching him watch her while she touched him exploringly.

His hands pressed down over hers, holding them where his heart beat roughly, quickly, at his rib cage.

"You don't even know what to do," he said half angrily. "Do you need an instruction manual?"

She blinked, feeling sanity come back with a rush. Her hands jerked back and she gasped. She moved away from him and sat up, grimacing as the movement caught her painfully. She could only imagine how she must look with her hair disheveled and her mouth swollen and her face flushed. Her eyes were like saucers.

He stared at her as if, for a moment, he didn't even recognize her. In fact, she hardly resembled the pale, composed woman he saw every day. He remembered her stinging comment and bending to kiss her in anger. Then the whole situation had gotten out of hand. How could he have forgotten himself so completely?

With a muffled curse, he got to his feet and fastened his shirt, straining to breathe normally. Of all the harebrained, stupid things he'd ever done . . . !

Jane was feeling equally addled. After that last sarcastic remark he'd made, he was going to be lucky if she ever spoke to him again! She picked up her book and opened it in her lap, refusing to even look at him. She was embarrassed, nervous and defensive because she'd been so vulnerable.

He finished snapping his shirt and tucked it back into his slacks. His hands were faintly unsteady, which made him furious. She got to him without even trying. He seemed to have no control whatsoever once he touched her. That had never happened with Marie, even in the early days of their romance. And she just sat there, so cool that butter wouldn't melt in her mouth, looking unaffected when he could barely breathe. That alone made him furious.

"Nothing to say?" he asked, glancing at her with steely gray eyes. "Would you like to repeat that bit about not finding me attractive?" he mocked.

She wouldn't look up. Her face reddened a little more, but otherwise, no expression showed in it. She didn't say a word.

He moved to the door. "I'll lock this behind me."

She nodded, but he wasn't looking.

He went out without another comment. His heart was still racing and he wasn't sure that his knees wouldn't buckle on the way to his car. Whatever Jane did to him, he hated it. He only wished he knew how to handle it. He had nothing to give her. It wasn't fair to lead her on when he felt that way. If she could be led on, that is. She'd been responsive enough until the last, when she'd seemed shocked and outraged. But she hadn't said a word. Not a word. He wondered what was going on in her mind.

He cursed as he fumbled the key into the ignition of his car and started it. Well, it didn't really matter what she thought, because that wasn't going to happen again. He'd have a good time with Micki and forget that Jane even existed.

Six

___

Only it didn't quite work out that way. Micki was a delightful companion, but when Todd held her while they were dancing, he felt nothing beyond a comfortable pleasure. The wild excitement that Jane engendered just by looking at him with her big blue eyes was totally missing.

"It was nice of you to invite me," Micki said with a smile. "But won't Jane mind?"

He scowled. "Jane is my employer," he said stiffly.

"Oh. Sorry. It was just that the way she looked..."

He pounced on that at once. "The way she looked...?" he prompted, and tried not to appear as interested as he was in her answer.

She laughed apologetically. "I thought she was in love with you," she explained.

His face was shot through with color. He stopped dancing. "That's absurd," he said slowly.

"Not really. You've obviously been kind to her," Micki continued, "and she was badly hurt in the wreck, wasn't she? I suppose it's inevitable that a woman will feel something for a man who helps her when she's in trouble. Mr. Kemble, her attorney, said that you've literally pulled her out of bankruptcy in a few short weeks and helped her get the ranch back on its feet."

He looked troubled. "Perhaps. The ranch had plenty of potential. It just needed a few modifications."

"Which you've accomplished. Jane is lovely, isn't she? Our advertising people are ecstatic about building a television campaign around her because she's so photogenic."

"She's easy enough on the eyes," he said noncommittally.

"And surprisingly modest about it. I've known of her for years, of course, since I grew up in Jacobsville. I'd heard that Dr. Coltrain gave up when you came to the Parker place. He's been going around with Jane for a long time. He's not a man I'd find easy to think of romantically, not with his temper, but Jane was fiery enough to stand up to him. Everyone thought they'd make a match of it eventually."

His face tautened. "Did they? Well, he only comes out to the place once in a while to check on her."

Micki hid a smile. "Oh, I see."

His broad shoulders shifted. "I'm certain that she could have gotten married long before this if she'd wanted to."

"I don't know. Most men seem to think a woman as lovely as Jane has more admirers than she can sort out, and a lot of pretty women don't even get asked out because of that perception. Actually I don't remember Jane dating anyone seriously. Except Dr. Coltrain, of course."

He was getting tired of hearing about Coltrain. "At her age, she's bound to have had a serious love affair."

"Do you think so?" Micki asked with studied carelessness. "If she has, it's been very discreet. Her reputation is impeccable."

He swung her around to the music. "What do you think of the band?" he asked with a pleasant smile.

She chuckled to herself. "It's nice, isn't it? I do enjoy a good two-step."

Todd was out of sorts by the time he drove Micki home, leaving her at the door with a chaste kiss before he sped back toward the ranch. It had been a pleasant evening, but he hadn't been able to get Jane's hungry kisses out of his mind. Then there was Micki's careless comment that she thought Jane was in love with him. That had set his mind spinning so that he took Micki back long before he normally would have.

When he drove away from her apartment house, it was barely eleven o'clock, and he was damned if he was going home that early. He stopped by a small bar out in the country and had a couple of beers before he drove the rest of the way out. By then it was almost one, and a more respectable hour for a man who'd enjoyed himself to be getting in.

He'd planned to go straight to the little house where he and Cherry were staying, but the lights were still on in the ranch house and he didn't see Tim's car out by the garage.

Frowning, and a little concerned, he went up to the front door and tried it. It was unlocked. Really worried now, he opened it and went in, closing it with a quiet snap and then working his way cautiously past the empty living room and study, down to the bedrooms.

There was light under only one door. He opened it and Jane gaped at him. She was sitting up in bed reading, wearing a low-cut blue satin gown with spaghetti straps. Her hair was loose around her shoulders and the firm, silky slopes of her breasts were bare almost to the nipples in her relaxed pose.

Lamplight became her, he thought helplessly. She was the most beautiful woman he'd ever seen. His whole body clenched at the thought of what lay under that silky fabric.

"Why the hell is the front door unlocked?" he asked shortly.

"It isn't," she faltered. "I locked it and left the lights on in case Meg needed to come in . . ."

"It wasn't locked. I walked right in. And they haven't come back. Did you check the answering machine?"

She frowned. "No. I took a couple of aspirin because my back was hurting, and then I lay down," she began.

He averted his eyes from her body. "I'll check for any messages." He went out, grateful for something besides the sight of her to occupy his mind. He went to the telephone in the living room and pressed the Play button on the answering machine. Sure enough, Tim had phoned to say that he and Meg would be spending the night with their daughter so that they could go to church with her the next morning. A distant relative was visiting and they wanted to get reacquainted.

He listened dimly as the machine reset itself and beeped. His heart was beating furiously in his chest. Two beers didn't usually affect him, but he hadn't eaten in a while and his head was reeling with the sight of Jane in that gown and what Micki had said about Jane being in love with him. What if he went into her bedroom and slid that silky gown off her breasts? Would she welcome him? If she loved him . . .

He muttered a curse and ran a hand through his damp hair. He should get out, right now, before he did something really stupid.

He got as far as the front door. He couldn't force himself to go through it. After a brief struggle with his conscience, he gave in to the pulsating need that was making him ache from head to toe. She could always say no, he told himself. But he knew that she wouldn't. Couldn't. He put on the locks, turned out the outside light and then the living room and study lights.

Jane had put down her book. When he walked back into her bedroom, she was sitting just where he'd left her, looking more vulnerable than ever.

"Did they...call?" she asked, her voice as choked as her body. She, too, was remembering the heated lovemaking of earlier in the evening and hungry for more of it. From the look on his hard face, so was he. She loved him so much that all thoughts of self-preservation had gone right out of her head in the hours since he'd left for his date. She had no pride left. Loneliness and love had eaten it away.

"They won't be home until morning," he said stiffly.

She looked at him with wide, helpless eyes, a little frightened and a little hungry. Everything she felt lay open to his searching eyes.

With a smile that was part self-contempt and part helpless need, he slowly closed and locked the bedroom door. He held her eyes while his hand went to snap off the main switch that controlled the bedside lamps.

The room went dark. She sat, breathing unsteadily, waiting. She saw the outline of him, big and threatening, as he came around the bed and slowly sat down beside her. Then she felt his lean, strong hands, warm on her arms as he slid the straps down and let the gown drop to her waist.

She felt herself shiver. Her breath caught. She felt the air on her body and the need for him was suddenly the most important thing in her life. She arched back with a faint moan, imploring, coaxing.

"I should be shot," he breathed. And then his warm mouth was on her soft, bare breasts, his hands gentle on her body as he eased her down on the bed.

She'd never known a man, but her responses were so acutely hungry that Todd didn't realize it at first. Her headlong acceptance of his deep kisses, of the caresses that grew more intimate as he eased her out of the gown and the faint briefs under it, made him too reckless to notice her shy hands on his chest.

She smelled of flowers and her body was the sweetest kind of warm silk under his mouth. He smoothed his lips over her from head to toe, enjoying her in a silence that trembled with sensation and sensuality.

When he was near the end of his patience, he divested himself of his clothing and drew her gently against the length of him. She caught her breath and tried to pull away, but his mouth on hers stilled the feeble protest.

"Are you using something?" he asked feverishly against her mouth.

"Wh... what?" she managed shakily.

"Are you on the Pill?" he persisted.

"N-no."

He groaned and reached down for his billfold. Thank God he was prepared. He'd never felt the blind need she kindled in his tall, fit body.

His question had almost brought Jane back to sanity as she realized the enormity of what she was doing, but his mouth found hers again, gently, while he did what was necessary. And the tender, passionate

kisses and caresses weakened her so that all she felt
was an aching emptiness that cried out to be filled.

"I'll be careful, baby," he whispered as he drew her
to him, on his side, so that he wouldn't jar or injure
her back. His long leg slid between hers and his hands
positioned her gently so that he could ease into intimacy with her. "Easy, now."

Her nails bit into his shoulders. She wanted him, but
it stung. She buried her mouth against his collarbone
and whimpered, but even then she didn't fight.

He wasn't so far gone that he didn't realize what was
wrong. He stilled, breathing roughly, his hands like
steel clamps on her slender hips. "Jane...?" he
whispered, shocked.

She was struggling to breathe. She moaned.

His powerful body shivered with the effort to hold
back, even for a space of seconds. "God, baby, I
didn't know...!" He groaned harshly. "I have to!
Forgive me, I can't stop! I can't!"

He surged against her, blind with a need as old as
time, as unstoppable as an avalanche.

There was a fierce flash of pain. She cried out. He
heard her in the back of his mind, and hated himself
for what was happening, but he was totally at the
mercy of the white-hot need in his loins. Tormented
seconds later, the painful tension in his body snapped
and blinding, furious pleasure lifted him to heights
he'd never known in his life. Then, he fell again to cold
reality and felt the guilt and anguish of the trembling
body containing his.

He kissed away the tears, his hands as gentle now as
they had been demanding only minutes before. "For-

give me," he whispered piteously. "Oh, Lord, I'm sorry! It was too late by the time I realized."

She lay her cheek against his cool, damp chest and closed her wet eyes. It had been painful and uncomfortable, and now her back was hurting again.

"You're twenty-five years old," he groaned, smoothing her hair. "What were you doing, saving it for marriage?"

"That isn't funny." She choked.

He drew in a sharp breath. "I suppose you were. You're so damned traditional."

She bit her lower lip. "Will you leave, please?"

He kissed her closed eyes. "No. Not until I give you what I had."

"I won't let you do that again!" she said hotly, hitting at him. "It hurt!"

His lips brushed against hers. He drew her hand to his mouth and kissed it, too. "The first time usually does, or so I'm told," he said gently. "But I can give you tenderness now."

"I don't want...!"

His mouth covered hers softly, slowly. He coaxed it to open to the lazy thrust of his tongue. His hands slid over her tense body, soothing her even as they began to incite her to passion. She didn't understand how it could happen. He'd hurt her. But she was moving closer to him. Her arms were lifting to enclose him. Her breasts were swelling under his hands and then his mouth, and she felt a tension building inside her that made her legs start to tremble.

He was gentle. He lay on his back and smoothed her body completely over him, deftly joining their bodies while he whispered soft, tender commands at her ear. His steely hands on her hips pulled and pushed and shifted her, so that she felt the fullness of him inside her building into an ache that blinded her with its promise.

She sobbed helplessly, clinging to him. "Oh...no," she whispered breathlessly as she felt her senses begin to climb some unbelievable peak.

"Don't fight it," he whispered at her temple. His voice was soft, but his breathing was quick and sharp, like the tug of his hard fingers and the thrust of his hips.

She whimpered as the pleasure caught her unaware and she stiffened on his body.

"Yes, that's it," he whispered feverishly. "That's it! Give in to me. Give in, Jane, give in! Let it happen!"

She heard her voice rising in sharp little cries as he increased the rhythm. Then, all at once, she went over an edge she hadn't expected, into realms of hot, black pleasure that took control of her body away from her brain and made her oblivious to everything except the hard heat of him filling her.

She pushed down as hard as she could and shuddered endlessly, frozen in pleasure, deaf and blind to the joyous laughter of the man holding her. Only when she was completely satisfied did he allow himself the exquisite pleasure of release.

He smoothed her long, damp hair over her spine and lay dreaming of the ecstasy he'd shared with her for a long time, until her faint weeping ceased and she lay still, trembling a little, on his spent body.

Her breasts were as soft as down. He shifted a little, so that he could feel them rubbing against his chest. His hands slid down to her hips, where they were still joined, and he pressed her closer into him.

She gasped. The touch of him was unbearably pleasurable, even now.

He mistook the gasp. "It's all right," he said gently. "You were protected, both times. I don't take that sort of risk, ever."

She was too embarrassed to know what to say. Her fingers clenched against him and she lay still, uncertain and hesitant in the aftermath.

He stretched stiffly and laughed. "But it was a near thing, I'll tell you that," he confessed. "Is your back all right?"

She bit her lip. "Yes."

He eased her onto her side and pulled away. Her teeth went deeper into her lip as reality fell on her like a cold brick.

He felt on the floor for her gown and briefs and laid them on her breasts. He bent and kissed her tenderly. "You'd better get your things back on," he whispered. "It's chilly."

She fumbled into them, listening to the rustle of fabric as he dressed by the side of the bed. She felt tears sting her eyes and hated herself for the one lapse of a lifetime. She hadn't even had the presence of mind to protect herself. Thank God he'd thought of it. And now there was the future to think of. How could she ever face him again, after this? He'd know how she felt about him. But whatever he felt was well concealed. He hadn't said a word while he was making love to her, except for soft commands and endearments. But there hadn't been one confession of love.

While she was worrying, he tucked her under the sheet and pushed her hair away from her face. "Sleep well," he said, trying not to betray how awkward he felt. Her cheek was wet. Did she hate him? Was she sorry? She'd tried to stop him, but he couldn't stop. Did she understand? Then, afterward, he'd wanted to make amends in the only way possible. He knew he'd given her pleasure, but would it be enough to make up for what he'd taken?

She turned her face away with a faint sigh and he left her. There would be time enough in the morning for talking, for explanations and apologies.

Jane was stiff and sore when she woke up. She opened her eyes and blinked from the brightness, and then she remembered. She sat up in bed, flushing with memories that made her feel hot all over.

She moved the top sheet away and grimaced at the betraying faint stains on the bottom one. She got out of bed and stripped away the sheet, throwing it on the floor, and her gown and briefs along with it. She went into the bathroom and showered herself from head to toe before she dressed in jeans and a round-neck yellow T-shirt and sneakers. Then she bundled up the laundry and put it into the washing machine, starting the load before Meg came in.

"Hey, that's my job," Meg complained gaily when she got home and found the drier running and another load of clothes going through the spin cycle in the washer.

"I didn't have anything to do," Jane said with a poker face and a smile. "Everyone's gone for the weekend except Todd. He was late getting in last night. He took Micki Lane to a dance."

"She's pretty," Meg said, frowning. "I thought maybe you liked him."

She shrugged. "He's very nice. I think he's a great accountant."

Nice. Meg sighed mentally at her dashed dreams of a romance between the two of them, and shooed her charge out of the kitchen while she saw to lunch.

But when Meg put it on the table, Todd still hadn't come to the house. Jane had been dreading it since dawn, uncertain of how she was going to face him. She was ashamed and embarrassed and a little afraid of having him taunt her with her helplessness.

"Where's Todd?" Meg asked when she had the salad and bread on the table.

"I don't know. I haven't seen him today," Jane said.

"It isn't like him to miss lunch." She went to the window and looked out. "His car's gone."

"Maybe he had a date with Micki today," Jane ventured, not looking up.

"Wouldn't he have said?"

Jane smiled. "He doesn't have to report to us."

"I guess not. Well, I'll call Tim and we'll eat."

It was a brief, pleasant lunch. Meg talked about their daughter and the distant cousin who'd come to visit. And if Jane was unusually silent, it went unremarked if not unnoticed.

* * *

Just before dark, Todd drove up with Cherry. Obviously, Jane thought, he'd gone up to Victoria to get her even though she'd said she was going to take the bus. Perhaps he was as uncomfortable as Jane now, only wanting to forget what had happened and needful of putting some space between them.

She was sitting on the sofa watching the news when they came in.

"How was your weekend?" Jane asked Cherry.

"Not very pleasant," Cherry said, without saying why. She smiled at Jane. "You look pale. Are you okay?"

She had to fight not to look at Todd. "I'm fine. I've had a lazy day."

"I need to check some figures. I'll take the books back over to the house with me, if you don't mind," he said, addressing Jane for the first time, his tone formal and remote.

"Of course," she said to his chin and even smiled. "Have you both eaten?"

"We had supper on the way," Todd said shortly. He went to get the books and came back with them tucked under one arm. "Say good-night, Cherry."

"Good night," the girl said obediently, aware of a new tension between the two adults in her life. She was too sensitive to mention it, though. And anyway, her dad had been quiet and unapproachable. Probably, she thought sadly, there had been another argument. It saddened her that her father and her new friend couldn't get along.

Jane called good-night and went back to her television program. She hadn't looked directly at Todd, or he at her. She wondered if things would ever be the same again.

The builders worked diligently at the repairs and finished right on schedule. Inspecting the new barn, Jane was amazed at their progress. It was a good job, too, not a slipshod effort.

The next step was to buy brood mares. Jane and Cherry went with Todd to an auction at a well-known horse ranch outside Corpus Christi. Todd and Jane looked at the catalog, not at each other, and Cherry enthused over each horse as it was led into the rink.

Jane had an excellent eye for horseflesh. Before her father's death, even he had deferred to her on buying trips. Todd quickly realized her ability, and he followed her father's example. They bought three good brood mares and a colt with excellent bloodlines. Todd arranged for them to be transported to the ranch and rejoined Cherry and Jane.

"Can we stop and get an ice cream on the way back?" Cherry asked, wiping away sweat. "It's awfully hot!"

"If Jane isn't too tired," he said stiffly.

"I'm fine," she said carelessly, putting an affectionate arm around Cherry. She was walking without her crutches now, although not as quickly as before. Two or three times, she'd had to fight the impulse to get on her horse and ride like the wind. Perhaps that was a realizable dream, but not just yet.

"Then we'll stop down the road a bit," Todd replied.

There was a small ice cream shop in a stand of mesquite trees, just off the main road. Although it was a bit isolated, there were plenty of cars surrounding it, and the small picnic area was full.

"We can sit under the trees," Cherry said. "Jane and I will grab the seats while you get the ice cream, Dad. I want a chocolate shake."

His head turned and he looked at Jane. "What would you like?" he asked politely.

"I'll have the same, thanks," she said, avoiding his eyes. She turned and walked away with Cherry.

Todd watched her hungrily. He'd handled the whole situation badly, and now he didn't know what to do. His conscience had tortured him over the past few days. He didn't sleep at night for it. He hadn't exactly forced her to do something she didn't want to, but she'd wanted him to stop and he couldn't. He'd taken away her right to give her chastity to a man she married. She might have loved him once, but he no longer thought she cared at all. She wouldn't look at him. If he came into a room, she found an excuse to leave it. She was subdued and withdrawn except when Cherry was around. And it was his fault. If only he hadn't touched her in the first place.

The man asked him again for his order and he snapped back to the present long enough to give it. He took the paper tray of milkshakes when the man came back and paid for them.

Minutes later, the three of them were sitting under the tree with the breeze playing in Jane's hair, sipping the cold, refreshing shakes.

"Don't you love chocolate?" Cherry said enthusiastically.

Jane smiled at her. "Yes, but it doesn't love me. Sometimes it gives me migraines."

"Why the hell didn't you say so?" Todd demanded angrily.

She glanced at him, startled by the venom in his tone. "I love chocolate."

"Which is no reason to deliberately bring on a headache."

She glared back at him. "I'll eat what I like. You're not my keeper!"

"Uh, what do you think of the colt, Jane?" Cherry interrupted quickly.

"What?" She was staring into Todd's furious eyes and he was staring back. The anger slowly began to fade, to be replaced by something equally violent, simmering, smoldering hot.

Cherry hid a smile. "I'll get some more napkins," she said.

Neither of them seemed to notice her leaving. Jane's face was getting redder by the second, and Todd's eyes narrowed until they were gray slits, full of heat and possession.

His hand reached out and caught hers hungrily. "Shall we stop pretending that nothing happened?" he asked roughly.

Seven

Jane felt his fingers contracting, intimately interlacing themselves with her own. She couldn't quite breathe normally, and her eyes were giving her feelings away.

"We've been dancing around it for days," he said huskily. He held her eyes searchingly. "I still want you," he added heavily. "More than ever."

She tore her gaze from his and looked down at their hands. "It shouldn't have happened."

"I know," he said surprisingly. "But it did. I've never had it that good, Jane. I think you and I could have a very satisfying relationship."

She looked up, but that wasn't love in his eyes. It was hunger, certainly. But it was an empty hunger.

"You mean, we could have an affair," she said quietly.

He nodded, dashing her faint hopes of something more. "I've tried marriage," he said bitterly. "I don't believe in it anymore. But you can't deny that we go up like fireworks when we're together. There won't be any consequences, any repercussions."

"What about Cherry?" she asked stiffly.

"Cherry's fourteen," he replied. "She knows that I'm no monk. She doesn't expect fairy-tale endings."

Her sad eyes searched his. "Doesn't she? I'm afraid that I do." She withdrew her hands from his.

His eyebrows arched. "You aren't serious, surely? You don't expect to marry a man and stay married for life, do you?" he added with a mocking laugh.

"Yes, I do, despite what...what happened the other night," she replied, her chin lifted proudly. "I'll be honest with him about it. But I do believe in love and I think people can stay together if they have common interests and they're willing to work at it."

He sat up straight, his mouth tightened into a thin line. "You don't think Marie and I worked at it?" he asked in a dangerously soft voice.

"It takes two people, committed..."

"Committed is the right word," he said on a harsh laugh. "People who get married should be committed!"

She saw then that his mind was closed on the subject, and all her hopes fell away. She smiled sadly. "I'm sorry. I don't have a bad marriage behind me, and I still believe in fairy tales. I don't want to have an affair with you, Todd."

His eyes glittered narrowly. "You loved what I did to you."

She shrugged, although it took her last bit of courage, and she smiled. "Sure I did. It was wonderful. Thanks."

He looked positively outraged. His high cheekbones flushed angrily and he opened his mouth to speak as Cherry came back with a handful of napkins.

"Here you go," she said, putting them down. "Isn't it nice here in the shade?"

Todd bit off what he was going to say. He finished his milkshake and got up. "We'd better get back," he said curtly. "I've got a lot of paperwork to catch up."

"But, Dad..." Cherry protested. She grimaced at the look he shot her. "Okay, okay, sorry!" She finished her milkshake with a wistful smile at Jane, and they all went back to the car.

The next few days were strained. Jane watched Cherry work with Feather and she conferred with Micki Lane about the plans for the advertising campaign.

"We'll need some publicity shots," Micki told her. "When can you come up to Victoria to do them?"

Jane picked a day and Micki offered to come and get her. "No, thanks," Jane said, "I'll have one of the hands run me up." She couldn't bear to see Micki with Todd.

"Oh. Well, okay," Micki said sadly. "How's Todd? I haven't heard from him lately."

"He's fine. Working hard, of course," she added matter-of-factly. "They're just finished putting up our new barn and he's been working closely with the contractor."

"I see," Micki said. She sounded happier. "I guess it takes up a lot of time, hmm?"

"A lot." More than he gave any other project, she thought, and probably it was just an excuse to keep out of Jane's way. Even Cherry was complaining about the fervor with which her father had approached the barn building and repairs.

"Then I'll see you Friday, yes?" Micki asked.

"Friday at nine," Jane agreed.

She didn't mention her trip to Todd or Cherry. She could ask Tim to drive her up, she was sure.

Meanwhile, she had to go to Dr. Coltrain for her checkup. He tested her reflexes, listened to her heart and lungs, checked her blood pressure and asked a dozen questions before he pronounced her blooming.

"Except for those bags under your eyes," he added, his piercing blue eyes on her drawn face. "Burke getting you down?"

She glared at him. "Todd Burke is none of your business."

He grinned at her. "I'm not blind, even if you are."

"What do you mean?"

"Oh, you'll find out one day." He leaned back in his chair and swiveled around. "Don't take it too fast, but I think you could start walking more."

"How about riding?"

He hesitated. "Slowly," he said. "For brief periods, and not on any of your usual mounts. That palomino gelding is gentle enough, I suppose. But don't overdo it."

"Bracket is gentle," she assured him. "He'd never toss me."

"Any horse will toss you under the right circumstances, and you know it."

She'd forgotten that he practically grew up on horseback. He rode as well as she did—better. He'd done some rodeo to help put himself through medical school.

"I'll be careful," she promised him.

"What's this I hear about you selling clothes?" he asked suddenly.

She grinned. "Meg told your mother, didn't she?" she asked. "I thought she would. I'm going to endorse a line of women's Western wear. It's very well made and I'll be on television and in magazines promoting it. In fact," she added, "I'm going up to Victoria on Friday to do the publicity photos for the magazines."

"How are you going to get there?"

"I thought I'd ask Tim ..."

"Ask me," he said with a slash of a grin. "I'm driving up to confer on a leukemia case at the hospital there. The patient is one of mine who moved away. You can ride with me."

"I may be there all day," she warned.

He shrugged. "I'll find something to keep me busy."

She smiled broadly. "Then I'd love to. Thanks."

"I'll pick you up at the ranch about eight-thirty. We can stop for coffee on the way."

"Okay. I'll look forward to it."

"How did you get here?"

"Meg dropped me off on her way to the grocery store. She'll be waiting in the parking lot. She only had a few things to get."

"Why didn't Burke bring you?" he asked.

She flushed. "Because I didn't ask him to!"

He pursed his lips. "I see."

She stood up. "No, you don't. Thanks for the ride. I'll see you in the morning."

"Jane."

She paused at the doorway, turning to meet his level gaze. "Do you need to ask me anything?"

She went scarlet, because she knew exactly what he meant. "No," she whispered huskily, "I do not!"

"Okay. No need to color up," he said gently, and smiled with affection. "But I'm here if you need me, and I'm not judgmental."

She drew in a slow breath. "Oh, Copper, I know that," she said miserably. "I wish..." she said huskily.

"No, you don't," he mused, smiling. "I had a case on you a few years ago, but our time passed. A blind man could see how you feel about Burke. Just be careful, will you? You're as green as spring grass, and that man knows his way around women."

"I'll be careful," she replied. "It's good to have a friend like you."

"That works both ways," he said.

There was a perfunctory knock on the door and Lou Blakely looked in. "Excuse me," she said with a glance at Jane, "Mr. Harris won't talk to me about his hemorrhoids. Could you . . . ?"

"I'll be with you in a minute," he said shortly.

She closed the door quickly.

"You're very rude to her, aren't you?" Jane remarked quietly. "She's a sweet woman. It hurts her when you snap, haven't you noticed?"

"Oh, yes," he said, and for a minute he didn't look like the man she knew. "I've noticed."

She let it drop, saying goodbye and pausing only to pay the receptionist before she went out to find Meg. Copper had been the kindest of boys when they were young, even though he was five years her senior. But he was different with Lou. He seemed to dislike her. Odd that he'd accepted her into his practice if he found her so irritating.

Meg drove Jane back to the ranch. She found Cherry waiting on the porch for her, beaming.

"I did it!" she told Jane excitedly. "I beat my old time! I wasn't even afraid! Oh, Jane, I've done it, I've overcome the fear! I can hardly wait for the next rodeo."

"I'm happy for you," Jane said with soft affection. "You're a great little rider. You're going to go far."

"I'll settle for being half as good as you," she said with worshiping eyes.

Jane laughed. "That won't be hard these days."

"Don't be silly. You'll always be Jane Parker. You've made your mark in rodeo already. You're famous! And you're going to be even more famous when you make those commercials."

"Well, we'll see. I'm not counting my chickens before they hatch!"

The photo session was the main topic of conversation at supper.

"I'll run you up to Victoria in the morning," Tim volunteered. "Or Todd might, if he can spare the time from that barn," he added, teasing the younger man, who was taciturn over his chicken and mashed potatoes and beans.

Todd looked up at Jane without any emotion. "If she wants me to, I don't mind," he said.

"Thank you both, but I have a ride," Jane said. She smiled. "Copper's got to go up there on a case, so he said I could go with him."

Todd didn't say a word, but the hand holding his fork stiffened. "The good doctor gets around, doesn't he?" he asked.

"Yes, he does. He's quite well-known in these parts. He graduated in the top ten percent of his class," she added. "He's very intelligent."

Todd, who'd never had the advantage of a college education, was touchy about it. He'd made millions and he was well-known in business circles, but there were still times when he felt uncomfortable around more educated businessmen.

"Dad's smart, too," Cherry said, as if she sensed her father's discomfort. "Even if he isn't a doctor, he's made lots of—"

"Cherry," her father said, cutting off the rest of her sentence.

"He's made lots of friends," Cherry amended, grinning cheekily at her parent. "And he's very handsome."

Jane wouldn't have touched that line with a pole. She finished her chicken and reached for her glass of milk.

"The chicken was great, Meg," she commented.

"It's nice to see everyone hungry again," Meg muttered. "I get tired of cooking for myself and Tim and Cherry."

"I guess the pain takes away your appetite sometimes, doesn't it, Jane?" Cherry asked innocently.

"Sometimes," she agreed, and couldn't look at Todd.

He tilted his coffee cup and drained it. "I'd better get back on the books."

"A couple of faxes came in for you today," Meg remarked. "One's from someone named Julia," she added with a twinkle in her eyes.

"Who's Julia?" Cherry asked, then her eyebrows lifted. "Oh. *Julia!*"

Her father's glance silenced her.

"I guess she's missing you, huh?" Cherry asked, grinning secretively.

"I don't doubt it," Todd agreed, thinking of the thousand and one daily headaches that Julia Emory was intercepting on his behalf while he lazed around in Jacobsville working for Jane. He put down his napkin. "I'd better get in touch with her. I'll, uh, reverse the charges," he assured Jane. "I wouldn't want to impose on my position here."

Jane only nodded. So he had other women. It shouldn't have come as a surprise. He was very handsome and fit, and she knew now why any woman would find him irresistible in bed. She flushed at her intimate memories of him and covered it by taking a large swallow of milk.

When Todd was gone, the conversation became more spontaneous and relaxed, but the room seemed empty.

"Did you ever think about marrying Dr. Coltrain?" Cherry asked Jane when Tim left and Meg started clearing away the supper things.

"Well, yes, I did, once," Jane confessed. "He's very attractive and we have a lot in common. But I never felt, well, the sort of attraction I'd need to feel to marry a man."

"You didn't want him in bed, in other words," Cherry said matter-of-factly.

"Cherry!"

"I don't live in a glass bottle," the young girl said. "I hear things at school and Dad's amazingly open about what I can watch on television. But I don't want to jump into any sort of intimacy at my age," she added, sounding very mature. "It's dangerous, you know. Besides, I have this romantic idea that it would be lovely to wait for marriage. Jane, did you know that some boys even feel that way?" she added with a giggle. "There's Mark, who goes to school with me, and he's very conservative. He says he'd rather wait and only do it with the girl he marries, so that they don't ever have to worry about STDs."

"About what?"

"Sexually transmitted diseases," she said. "Honestly, Jane, don't you watch television?"

Jane cleared her throat. "Well, obviously I haven't been watching the right programs, have I?"

"I'll have to educate you," the girl said firmly. "Didn't your parents tell you anything?"

"Sure, but since I never liked a boy enough..." She hesitated, thinking about how it had been with Todd, and her face colored.

"Oh, I see. Not even Dr. Coltrain?" she asked.

Jane shook her head.

"That's really sad."

"I'll find someone, one of these days," Jane assured her, and looked up, right into Todd's quiet, interested eyes.

"Hi, Dad! I've been explaining sex to Jane." She shook her head as she got up. "Boy, and I thought I was backward! See you later, Jane, I'm going to saddle up Feather!"

She ran out the door, leaving Todd alone with Jane, because Meg was in the kitchen rattling dishes as she loaded the dishwasher.

"Do you need a fourteen-year-old to explain sex to you?" he asked quietly. "I thought you learned all you needed to know from me."

She bit her lower lip. "Don't."

He moved closer, a sheaf of papers in one lean hand, and stood beside her chair. "Why deny us both the kind of pleasure we shared?" he asked. "You want me. I want you. What's wrong with it?"

She looked up into his eyes. "I want more than a physical relationship," she said.

He reached down and touched her cheek lightly. "Are you certain?" he said softly.

She grimaced and tried to look away, but he caught her chin and held her flushed face up to his eyes.

"So beautiful," he murmured. "And so naive. You want the moon, Jane. I can't give it to you. But I can give you pleasure so stark that you bite me and cry out with it."

She put her fingers against his hard mouth. "You mustn't!" she whispered frantically, looking toward the kitchen.

He caught her wrist and pulled her gently up out of the chair and against him, so that they were touching all the way up and down. "Meg wouldn't be embarrassed if she saw us kissing. No one would, except you." His hand tightened, steely around her fingers as he used his grip to force her even closer. Something untamed touched his face, glittered in his eyes as he looked down at her. His mouth hovered just above her lips. "You can deny it all you like, but when I hold out my arms, you'll walk into them. If I offer you my mouth, you'll take it. You're a puppet on a string, baby," he whispered seductively, letting the word arouse explosive memories in her mind.

She meant to protest. She wanted to. It was just that his hard mouth was so close. She could feel its warmth, taste the minty scent of it on her parted lips. Of course she wanted to deny what he was saying. What *was* he saying?

He bent a fraction of an inch closer. "It's all right," he whispered, moving his hips lazily against her, so that she trembled with kindling fevers. "Take what you want," he challenged.

She was sure that she hated him. The arrogant swine...

But all she wanted to do was kiss him, and it was a shame to waste the opportunity. It was so easy to reach up to him, to pull his hard mouth onto hers and feel its warm, slow pressure. It was so sweet to press her slender body into his and feel his swift, unashamed arousal.

He wasn't even holding her. His free hand was in her hair, savoring its silky length while she kissed him hungrily, passionately. He tasted of coffee and he smelled of spicy cologne. He was clean and hard and warm and she loved the feel of his powerful body against hers. Her legs began to tremble from the contact and she wondered if they were going to support her for much longer.

It was a moot point. Her nearness was as potent to him as his was to her. Seconds later, he put the papers on the table and wrapped her up in his arms, so that not a breath separated them. His mouth opened, taking hers with it, and his tongue pushed deep inside her mouth in a slow, aching parody of what his body had done to hers that long night together.

She moaned with the onslaught of the pleasure, trembling in his arms as the kiss went on and on.

His hands slid up and down her sides until they eased between and his thumbs worked lazy circles around her taut breasts. He remembered the taste of them in his mouth, the warm envelope of her body encircling him in the darkness. One hand went to her hips and gathered her against him roughly, and she cried out at the stab of discomfort in her hip.

The sound shocked him into lifting his head. His eyes were blank with aroused ardor, but all at once they focused on her drawn face.

"Did I hurt your back?" he asked huskily.

"A little," she whispered.

"I'm sorry." He brushed the hair away from her face. "I'm sorry, baby. I wouldn't hurt you for all the world, don't you know that?"

"You did..." she blurted.

His eyes glittered. "Yes. God, yes!" He actually shivered. "I didn't know until I'd torn you, there..." His eyes closed and he shivered again with the memory. "I thought I might die of the pleasure, and the shame, because you asked me to stop and I couldn't." His mouth smoothed softly over hers. "You don't know what it's like, do you, to want someone past reason, past honor? I wanted you like that. I would have killed to have you, in those few blind seconds that robbed me of reason. I was ashamed, Jane," he breathed into her mouth, "but I was too excited to pull away. I'm sorry."

She closed her eyes, drinking in the feel of him. "It's all right. Afterward—" she hesitated, and her body clenched at the memory of afterward "—I...I think I understood."

His mouth was hot on her eyelids, her cheeks, her chin. "I thought you were never going to stop convulsing," he whispered. "I remember laughing with the pure joy of it, knowing that I'd given you so much pleasure."

"So that was why...!"

"Yes." His hands framed her face and he looked deep into her eyes. "Come to bed with me tonight. I'll give you that pleasure again, and again. I'll make love to you until you fall asleep in my arms."

She wanted to. Her eyes told him that she wanted to. But despite the pleasure she remembered, she also remembered his easy rejection of her when his passion was spent. He'd left her as soon as he was finished, with no tenderness, no explanations, no apologies. He wanted her now, desperately. But when he was satisfied, it would be the same as it had been before, because he only wanted her. He didn't love her. He was offering her an empty heart.

She closed her eyes against the terrible temptation he offered. That way lay self-destruction, no matter how much temporary relief he gave her.

"No," she said finally. "No, Todd. It isn't enough."

He scowled. She was trembling against him. Her mouth was swollen and still hungry for his, her arms still held him.

"You don't mean that," he accused gently.

She opened her eyes and looked up at him. "Yes, I do," she said quietly. She pulled away from him, slowly, and stepped back. "You're handsome and sexy, and I love kissing you. But it's a dead end."

"You want promises," he said shortly.

"Oh, no," she corrected. "Promises are just words. I want years of togetherness and children." Her face softened as she thought of a little girl like Cherry, or perhaps a baby boy. "Lots of children."

His face went rigid. "I have a child."

She searched his eyes. "Yes, I know. She's a wonderful girl. But I want one of my own, and a husband to go with them."

He was seething with unsatisfied passion and anger. "Wouldn't it be a great world if we all got exactly what we wanted?"

"It certainly would." She moved away from him, concentrating on each breath. She held on to the back of her chair. "And maybe I never will. But my dreams are sweet," she added, lifting her eyes. "Much sweeter than a few weeks of lust that end with you walking right out of my life."

His face went even harder. "Lust?"

"Without love, that's all sex is."

"You little hypocrite," he accused flatly, and reached for her. He was kissing her blindly, ardently, when the door opened and a shocked Cherry stopped dead in the doorway.

Eight

Todd lifted his head, freezing in place, while Jane gently pushed away from him, red-faced.

"Sorry," Cherry murmured, and then grinned. "I was looking for Meg. Don't let me interrupt anything."

She darted past them into the kitchen and closed the door pointedly.

"I'm sorry," Todd said curtly, pushing his hair off his forehead. "That was a stupid thing to do."

Jane didn't know what stupid thing he meant, so she didn't reply. She moved away from him and sat down, her back aching from the unfamiliar exercise. He hesitated for a few seconds, but he couldn't think of a single defense for his uncharacteristic behavior.

"Excuse me," he said, picking up the papers from the table. "I'd better get to work."

He left her sitting there, and he didn't look back on the way out. Cherry came in a few minutes later, and grimaced when she saw that Jane was alone.

"I didn't mean to burst in," Cherry told her. "I didn't expect ... Gosh, I never saw Dad kiss anyone like that! Not even my mother, when I was little!"

Jane flushed. "It was just a ... mistake," she faltered.

"Some mistake. Wow!" She chuckled. Her whole face lit up. "Do you like him?"

"Don't start building dreams on me and your father," Jane said somberly. "There's no future in it. He doesn't want marriage and I don't want anything else," she added flatly.

Cherry's face fell. "Oh."

"You're still my friend, Cherry," she said with a smile. "Okay?"

Cherry's mouth curled down but after a minute she smiled back. "Okay."

Jane went up to Victoria with Copper and spent most of the day posing in various articles of SlimTogs for the photographer. He was nice, and very helpful, and considerate of Jane's back problem. It was worse today because of Todd's ardor the night before, but Jane wasn't about to mention that to anybody. It was only a twinge, anyway.

"That should wrap it up," Micki said a few minutes later, after she'd talked to the photographer. "Jack said that he got some great shots. We'll make our selection for the layout and then we'll be in touch with you. There may be a couple of promotional appearances, by the way, at a rodeo and maybe for the opening of one of our new stores. We'll let you know."

"It was fun," Jane said. "I enjoyed it. And I really do like the clothes."

"We like you," Micki said with a nice smile. "You're a good sport. Uh, Todd didn't come up with you, did he?"

She shook her head. "He's still up to his neck with projects on the ranch. My own men answer to him, now, not to me. I'm going to have a hard time getting control back when he leaves."

"Is he leaving?"

"Not anytime soon, I don't think," Jane replied. She hated Micki's probing questions, but she couldn't afford to say so and reveal her own feelings for the man.

"He's very attractive," Micki said, her smile wistful and a little sad. "I guess he's got plenty of girlfriends."

"I don't doubt it," Jane replied. "They even fax him letters," she said absently.

Micki chuckled. "Well, that lets me out of the running, I suppose. You're not sweet on him yourself, are you?" she added curiously.

"I'd have to get in line," Jane said. "And I'd be a long way back."

"Just our luck, isn't it? A dreamy man like that doesn't come along every day, but there's always a woman in possession, I guess." She shook her head. "I think I'm destined to be an old maid."

"Marriage isn't everything," Jane said. "You might become the head of your corporation."

"Anything's possible. But I have a secret, sinful hunger for dirty dishes and ironing a man's shirts and having babies. Shameful, isn't it? Don't tell anyone."

"You closet housewife, you!"

Micki chuckled. "I love what I do, and I make a lot of money. I can't complain. It's just that once in a while I don't want to live alone."

"Who does?" Jane asked. "But sometimes we don't have a choice."

"So they say. I'll be in touch soon, okay? Have a nice trip home."

"Thanks."

Jane went downstairs and phoned the hospital. Copper drove over to pick her up. But instead of heading home, he took her to Victoria's nicest restaurant for supper.

"But I'm not dressed properly," she protested, gesturing toward her chambray blouse and matching long skirt.

"Neither am I." He was wearing a sport jacket and a knit shirt with his slacks. "They can stare if they like. Can't they?"

She laughed. "All right, then. I'd be delighted to have dinner with you, if you don't mind the casual clothes."

"I never minded."

He took her inside the swanky restaurant, where he ordered her meal—lobster and steak and salad, topped off with an ice-cream-covered brownie.

"I'll have sweet dreams about that dessert for years," she murmured on the way home.

"So will I."

She turned her head toward him. He was single-minded when he drove. Probably he was like that when he operated, too. He specialized in diseases of the lung, and he was a surgeon of some note. He occasionally was called in to operate in the big city hospitals. But in recent years, he stayed close to home. He was mysterious in many ways. An enigma.

"Do you want children?" she asked suddenly.

He chuckled. "Sure. Are you offering?"

She flushed. "Don't be silly."

He glanced at her. "Say the word. I'm willing if you are. I like kids and I wouldn't balk at marriage. We've got more in common than a lot of people."

"Yes, we have. But there's just one thing missing."

He smiled ruefully. "And I know what it is."

"Two out of three isn't bad."

"No," he agreed. "But I couldn't live with a woman who suffered me in bed, Jane. That would be impossible."

"I know." She reached across the seat and slid her hand into his where it rested on the gearshift. "I'm sorry. I wish I felt that way."

His fingers contracted. "You do. But with Burke, not me."

She didn't deny it. She leaned her head against the headrest. "He wants to have a blazing affair and then go back to Victoria."

"What do you want?"

"Marriage. Children. Forever after."

"He might want those things, too, after he got used to you."

"He might get tired of me."

"Life doesn't come with guarantees," he said gently. He glanced at her drawn, unhappy face. "You have a history of migraine. I wouldn't dare prescribe birth control pills for you, because of that. But there are other tried-and-true methods."

"Copper!"

He held on to her hand. "Grow up. We don't always get the brass ring. That doesn't mean we can't get some pleasure out of the ride. At least you'd have some sweet memories."

"I'm surprised at you," she said.

He glanced at her. "No, you're not. And I'm not surprised or disappointed in you for being human. Sex is a natural, beautiful part of life. It's very rare that two people love each other enough to experience its heights. Burke may not want to marry you, honey, but he loves you."

"What!"

"I think you know it, too, deep down. He's pretty readable to another man. He was jealous of me the first time he saw me."

"That could be sexual jealousy."

"It could have been. But it wasn't. He's too protective of you." He patted her hand gently. "He had a bad marriage, didn't he, and he's probably afraid to take another chance. But if he cares enough, eventually he'll give in. Isn't it worth fighting for?"

"Fighting for." She grimaced. "I can't. I just can't. That . . . belongs in marriage."

"I couldn't agree more. It does. But, then, from my point of view, marriage is just a matter of time. He loves you. You love him. And he strikes me as a pretty conventional fellow. He has a daughter to think of, too."

"He says he'll never marry again."

"The president said he wouldn't raise taxes."

She looked at him and burst out laughing. "Don't compromise your principles," he advised. "But you can keep him interested without tearing your clothes off for him."

"I suppose so."

"Now, tell me about this ad promotion."

She did, glad to talk about some subject less complicated than Todd Burke.

When they got home it was well after dark and Todd was in the house with Meg, pacing the floor.

He went out to meet Jane as she came up the steps, having thanked Copper and waved goodbye.

"Where have you been?" he demanded.

She lifted both eyebrows. "Having lobster and steak."

"And then?" he challenged angrily.

"And then," she whispered, leaning close, "we got into the back seat and made love so violently that all four tires went flat!"

He stared at her long and hard and then suddenly laughed. "Damn you!"

She went close to him, putting both hands against his shirtfront. "I couldn't make love with anyone except you," she said, living up to her new resolve to tell him nothing but the truth, always. "I love you."

His heart ran away. She was the very picture of femininity, and the sight of her long hair made him ache to feel it against his bare chest, as he had the night they loved each other. He gathered up a handful of it and drew it to his cheek.

"I love you, too," he said unexpectedly. His breath sighed out at her temple while she stood still against him, unbelieving. "I loved you the night I took you." He kissed her eyelids closed. "People can't satisfy each other that completely unless they love, didn't you know?"

"No," she whispered, stunned by the revelation.

His mouth moved gently down to her soft lips and traced them. "Won't you change your mind?" he asked huskily.

Her hands clenched on his shirtfront. "Copper won't give me the Pill because I have a history of migraines," she said bluntly.

His body froze in position. "You talked to that cowboy doctor about the Pill?"

"No, he talked to me about it! He knows that I love you."

He didn't know how to take it. For a moment, anger overshadowed what she was saying. And then, all at once, understanding pushed its way into his mind.

He moved back, frowning. "You can't take the Pill?"

"That's right. So the risk of a child would always be there. I couldn't...do anything about it, if I got pregnant," she added firmly. "And since I feel so strongly about it, I don't want to take any more chances with you. I didn't...that is, nothing happened last time."

"I took precautions," he said stiffly.

"Yes, I know. But accidents happen."

His hands stilled on her shoulders. He was quiet, thoughtful. A child with Jane would be a disaster. He couldn't walk away from a child. He could picture a little girl with long blond hair and big blue eyes in a taffeta dress. He could take her to birthday parties, as he'd taken Cherry when she was little. Or there might be a little boy, whom he and Jane could teach to ride. A son.

"You're very quiet," she remarked.

"Yes."

"I'm sorry," she said, lifting her eyes to his. "But it's better not to start things we can't finish. And I'd be the last person in the world who'd want to trap you."

He searched her sad eyes. His fingers touched her lower lip, testing its softness. "Marie didn't want to make a baby with me," he said roughly. "We were both drunk and I knew she was on the Pill. But she'd forgotten to take it a few times. That's the only reason Cherry was conceived."

"For heaven's sake!"

"Are you shocked?" he asked lazily. "Jane, she didn't want a child. Some people don't."

"Yes, I know, but now she loves Cherry."

"So do I. With all my heart. And the day she was born, when they put her into my arms, I cried like a boy. It was unbelievable to have a child of my own."

The awe and wonder of the experience touched his eyes just briefly, before he banished it. He looked down at Jane and his hands cradled her hips. "Even if I were...willing—which I'm not," he added curtly, "you won't be able to carry a child, not for a long time." He grimaced. "And as you say, the risk would always be there, if you couldn't take the Pill. But you were willing to take any risk with me that night," he reminded her.

"Yes, but it didn't happen," she said curtly. "Nothing happened afterward!"

Her tone startled him. She sounded disappointed.

He didn't speak for a minute. His eyes searched her downcast face. "Jane ... you wanted to get pregnant, didn't you?"

She bit her lower lip almost through and pulled away from him. "What I wanted is nobody's business except my own, and it's a good thing that you aren't forced into doing something you'd hate."

"Maybe so. But . . ."

She laughed. "Don't look so somber. Everything's all right. You'll go back to your job in Victoria and I'll make a fortune selling clothes with my name on them. We'll both do fine."

"Will you marry Coltrain?" he asked bluntly.

"I don't love him," she said sadly. "If I did, I'd marry him in a minute."

"Marriages have succeeded on less."

"And ended on more."

He couldn't debate that. He touched her lips with his. "I won't stop wanting you. If you change your mind, you only have to say so."

"I can't. I can't, Todd." She moved away and left him standing there. He wanted her, that was obvious, but he'd hate her if anything happened. He'd marry her, certainly, if there was a child. But it would be a hateful relationship. She didn't want him that way.

The next Friday, Todd drove Cherry up to Victoria to spend another weekend with her mother. He stayed in town, too, to get some of his own impending paperwork out of the way and to keep his mind off Jane. The hunger he felt for her was becoming a real problem.

Cherry waved goodbye to him from her mother's elegant front porch. The house Marie shared with William, her second husband, was a startling white restored Victorian, with gingerbread woodwork and a gazebo on a spotless manicured lawn. It had all the warmth of a photograph, but it suited a woman who was trying to build an interior design business in south Texas.

"Your father seemed very out of sorts," Marie remarked as she and Cherry went inside.

"I think it's because of Jane," the girl replied with a grin. "I caught them kissing, and I mean kissing!" she added, shaking her hand with appropriate facial expressions.

Marie made a curt movement. "Todd has said repeatedly that he doesn't want to marry again," she said.

"Never say never," Cherry murmured and grinned. "Jane's been helping me with my turns. She says I'm just the picture of elegance on horseback. I wish I could be more like her," she said, without realizing how dreamy she sounded. "She's so beautiful, and everyone knows who she is in rodeo. She's going to endorse some women's Western wear. They'll have her on TV and in magazines... Gosh, it's so exciting!"

Marie wasn't jealous of Todd anymore. Their marriage was history. But she was jealous of her only daughter, who now seemed to be transferring all her loyalties to a disabled rodeo star with a reputation that was already fading. She didn't like it one bit.

"I thought we might go shopping again tomorrow," Marie ventured.

Cherry started to speak and ended in a sigh. "All right."

"You should love pretty clothes, at your age," Marie said, clinging desperately to the only real common desire they still shared, a love of clothes.

"I do, I guess," Cherry said. "Rodeo clothes, at least. But I'd love some new books on horses and medicine."

"Books! What a waste of time!"

Cherry's eyebrows arched. "Mother, I'm going to be a surgeon."

Marie patted her shoulder gently. "Darling, you're very young. You'll change your mind."

"That isn't what Jane says, when I tell her about wanting to practice medicine," Cherry said sharply.

Marie glared at her. "And that's quite enough about Jane," she said sarcastically. "I'm your mother. You don't talk back to me."

Cherry's mouth pulled down. "Yes, ma'am."

Marie smoothed over her perfect coiffure. "Let's have tea. I've had a very hectic morning."

Doing what, arranging the flowers? Cherry thought irritably, but she only smiled and didn't say another word. Compared to Jane, who was always doing something or reading about ranching or genetics, Marie was very dull stuff indeed. Her life seemed to be composed of clothes and society, and she had no interests past them.

Her father, like Jane, had an active mind and he fed it constantly with books and educational television. Cherry remembered her parents being together very rarely during her childhood, because Marie didn't like horses or riding, or reading, or computers. Cherry and her father shared those interests and that had formed an early bond between them. Now Jane, also, shared the same interests. Cherry wondered if her father ever noticed. He seemed very attracted to Jane physically, but he paid little attention to her leisure pursuits. She'd have to get them together long enough to push them into really talking.

Remembering the pleasure in Jane's face when she'd said she was going to Victoria with Dr. Coltrain brought Cherry up short. The doctor would be formidable competition for her father. She'd have to see if she couldn't do something to help. The more she thought about having Jane for a stepmother, the happier she became.

Marie and William had an engagement Saturday night, so she decided to run Cherry back to the ranch early that afternoon. She phoned Todd at the office to tell him that she'd drop the girl off, but he was involved in a business meeting so Miss Emory took the message and promised to relay it.

Marie smiled to herself as she and Cherry got into her silver Mercedes. Somehow she was going to throw a spanner into Todd's spokes and prevent her daughter from becoming lost to the competition. She already had a good idea of how to do it, too.

"Does Jane know that your father is rich?" she asked Cherry.

"Heavens, no," Cherry said, defending her idol. "She doesn't even know that he owns a computer company. All Dad has told her is that he keeps the books for a company in Victoria."

"My, my. Why the subterfuge?"

"Well, Dad felt sorry for Jane," she said without thinking that she might be betraying her father to her mother. "She hurt her back in a wreck and she could barely walk. The ranch was in trouble. She didn't have anyone who could manage money to help her. So on an impulse, Dad offered to take over the manager's job. You wouldn't believe what he's done for her. He's improved the property, bought livestock, got her into a licensing venture with that clothing manufacturer— all in a few weeks. I heard him say that the ranch is going to start paying back the investment any day now."

"Where did she get the money to do all that? Has she got money of her own?" Marie asked with studied carelessness.

"Oh, no, she was flat broke, Dad said. He went to the bank and stood good for a loan to make the improvements. She doesn't know."

Ammunition, Marie was thinking. "Tell me about Jane," Marie coaxed.

It didn't take much to get Cherry talking about the woman she worshiped. In the drive to Jacobsville, she told Marie everything she knew. By the time they reached the Parker ranch, Marie had enough to put the skids under the former rodeo queen and get back her daughter's loyalty.

"I do wish you'd consider spending the rest of the summer with me," Marie said as they pulled up at the front door. "We could go to Nassau or down to Jamaica. Even to Martinique."

"I'd love to, but I have to practice for the rodeo in August," Cherry explained. "I really need to work on my turns."

"Oh...horses!" Marie muttered. "Such a filthy hobby."

"They're very clean, actually. There's Jane!"

Marie got out of the car and studied the woman approaching them. Jane was wearing jeans and a pink T-shirt. Her blond hair was in a braid down her back and she wasn't wearing any makeup, but that didn't lessen her beauty. If anything, it enhanced it. She was slender and elegant to look at, and she had grace of carriage despite her injury. She was twice as pretty as Marie. The other woman, at least ten years Jane's senior, had no difficulty understanding Todd's interest and Cherry's devotion to the woman. Marie hated her on sight.

"Jane, this is my mother. Mom, this is Jane," Cherry introduced them, beaming.

"I've heard so much about you," Marie said with reserved friendliness. "How nice to meet you at last, Miss Parker."

"Call me Jane, please," the other woman said kindly. She slid a welcoming arm around Cherry, who smiled up at her with the kind of affection she used to show her mother. It made Marie go cold inside. "I've missed you," she told Cherry.

"I've missed you, too," Cherry said warmly.

"Would you like tea, Mrs. . . . ."

"Oh, call me Marie. Yes, I'd love a cup," Marie said formally.

Jane grimaced. "I meant a glass of iced tea, actually."

"That would be fine."

"Come in, then."

Jane led the way into the spacious living room. Marie's keen eye could see dozens of ways to improve it and make it elegant, but she bit down on her comments. She wanted to worm her way into Jane's confidence and criticizing the decor wasn't going to accomplish that.

"Could you ask Meg to fix some tea and cookies on a tray?" Jane asked Cherry.

"Sure! I'll be right back!"

She was gone and Marie accepted Jane's offer of a seat on the wide, comfortably upholstered sofa.

"Well, you're not at all what I expected," Marie began with a kind smile. "When my husband—excuse me, my *ex*-husband," she amended sweetly, "told me that he'd taken a little job down in Jacobsville to help a poor crippled woman, I had someone older in mind!"

Nine

———

At first Jane thought that she might have misheard the other woman. But when she leaned forward and looked into Marie's cold eyes, she knew that she hadn't.

"I'm not crippled," Jane said proudly. "Temporarily slowed down, but not permanently disabled."

"Oh. I'm sorry. I must have misunderstood. It doesn't matter. Whatever your problem is, Todd felt sorry for you. He's a sucker for a hard-luck story. Amazing, isn't it," she added, watching Jane as she played her trump card, "that a multimillionaire, the head of an international corporation, would sacrifice his vacation to get an insignificant little horse ranch out of the red."

Jane didn't move, didn't breathe, didn't flinch. She stared at the older woman blankly. "I beg your pardon?"

Marie's pencil-thin brows rose. "You didn't know?" She laughed pleasantly. "Well, how incredible! He's been featured in God knows how many business magazines. Although, I don't suppose you read that sort of thing, do you?" she added, allowing her eyes to pause meaningfully on the latest issue of a magazine on horsemanship.

"I don't read business magazines, no," Jane said. She touched her throat lightly, as if she felt choked.

"Todd must have found it all so amusing, pretending to be a simple accountant," Marie said, leaning back on the sofa elegantly. "I mean, what a comedown for him! Living like this—" she waved a careless arm "—and driving that pitiful old sedan he borrowed. Honestly, he had to have the chauffeur drive the Ferrari and the Rolls twice a week just to keep them from getting carbon on the valves."

Rolls. Ferrari. Multimillionaire. Jane felt as if she were strangling. "But he keeps the books," she argued, trying desperately to come to grips with what she was being told.

"He's a wizard with figures, all right," Marie said. "He's an utter genius at math, and without a college education, too. He has a gift, they say."

"But, why?" she groaned. "Why didn't he tell me the truth?"

"I suppose he was afraid that you might fall in love with his bank account," Marie said with a calculating glance. "So many women have, and you were a poverty case. Not only that, a crippled poverty case. You might have thought he was the end of the rainbow."

Jane's face went rigid. She got to her feet slowly. "I make my own way," she said coldly. "I don't need any handouts, or anybody's pity."

"Well, of course you don't," Marie said. "I'm sure Todd would have told you the truth, eventually."

Jane's hands clenched by her side. She was white.

The sound of running footsteps distracted Marie.

"Meg says she'll bring the— Jane! What is it?" Cherry asked as she entered the room, concerned. "You look like you've seen a ghost!"

"Yes, you are very pale," Marie said. She glanced worriedly at her daughter. She hadn't counted the cost until now. Cherry was looking at her with eyes that grew steadily colder.

"What did you say, Mother?" she asked her parent.

Marie got up and clasped her hands in front of her. "I only told her the truth," she said defensively. "She'd have found out anyway."

"About Dad?" Cherry persisted. When Marie nodded, Cherry's face contorted. She looked at Jane and felt the older woman's pain and shock all the way to her feet.

Marie was feeling less confident by the second. Cherry's eyes were hostile and so were Jane's. "I should go, I suppose," Marie began.

"That might be a very good idea, Mother," Cherry said icily. "Before Dad comes home."

Another complication Marie hadn't considered. She gnawed her lower lip. "I never meant to . . ."

"Just go," Jane snapped.

"And the sooner the better," Cherry added.

"Don't you talk to me that way! I'm your mother!" Marie reminded her hotly.

"I'm ashamed of that," Cherry said harshly. "I've never been so ashamed of it in all my life!"

Marie's indrawn breath was audible. Her pale eyes filled with sudden tears. "I only wanted..." she began plaintively.

Cherry turned her back. Marie hesitated only for a moment before she scooped up her purse and went quickly to the front door. The tears were raining down her cheeks by the time she reached the Mercedes.

Inside the house, Jane was still trying to subdue her rage. She sat down again, aware of Cherry's worried gaze.

"Is what she said true? That your father owns a computer company, that he has a Ferrari and a Rolls and he's spending his vacation getting my ranch out of debt because he feels sorry for me?" Jane asked the girl.

Cherry groaned. "Oh, it's true, but it's not like that! Mother's just jealous because I talk about you so much. I guess I upset her when I made her realize how little we had in common. It's all my fault. Oh, Jane...!"

Jane took another steadying breath and folded her hands in her lap. "I wondered," she said absently. "I mean, with a brain like that, why would he still be working for somebody else, at his age. I've been a fool! He played me like a radio!"

"He didn't do it to hurt you," Cherry argued. "Jane, he just wanted to help. And then, after we'd been here for a while, he didn't know how to tell you. I'm sure that's why he hasn't said anything. He cares for you."

Cares. He'd said that he loved her. *But you don't keep secrets from people you love,* she was thinking. He'd lied by omission. He'd let her fall in love with him, and he had to know that there was no future for them. If he'd been a simple accountant, perhaps it would have worked out. But he was a multimillionaire, a powerful businessman. What would he want with a little country girl from south Texas who only had a high school education and no social skills? She wouldn't know what to do with herself at a society party. She wouldn't even know what utensils to use. And she was a rancher. Her eyes closed as the reality closed in on her.

"Talk to me," Cherry pleaded.

Jane couldn't. She gripped her legs hard as she fought with her demons. Todd was coming back today. She'd have to face him. How would she be able to face him, with what she knew?

Then the solution occurred to her. *Copper*. She could invite Copper over for supper, and play up to him—if she warned Copper first that she was going to—and she could put on a good act. It had all been a mistake, she hadn't meant what she said about loving him, she was lying...

"I don't want your father to know that your mother told me the truth," Jane said after a minute. Her blue eyes met Cherry's gray ones evenly. "I'll talk to him later."

"Mother's not vindictive, really," Cherry said in her mother's defense. "She's just shallow, and jealous. It's funny, really, because she doesn't even know how to talk to me. Not like you do. Please don't hate me because of this, Jane."

"Cherry!" Jane was genuinely shocked. "As if I could hate you!"

The young face softened. Cherry smiled. "We're still friends?"

"Certainly we are. None of this has anything to do with you and me."

"Oh, thank goodness," she said heavily.

"It's just as well, really," Jane continued without looking directly at Cherry, "because I'd decided that things wouldn't work out with your father and me, anyway. He isn't really the rancher type."

Cherry frowned. "But he comes from ranching people in Wyoming. He grew up around horses and cattle."

"Still, he doesn't spend much time with them now," Jane insisted. "If he's the president of a company, then he lives in the fast lane. I don't. I can't."

Cherry saw all her dreams coming apart. "You could get to know him better before you decide that you can't."

Jane smiled and shook her head. "No. You see, Dr. Coltrain and I were talking the other day. Copper's like me, he's from Jacobsville and his family has lived here as long as mine has. We're suited to each other.

In fact," she lied, "I've invited him for supper to-night."

"You didn't tell me," Cherry protested.

"I didn't know you'd be here, did I?" she asked, and sounded so reasonable that Cherry was totally fooled. "For all I knew, your father was going to drive up to Victoria to get you tomorrow."

"Yes, that's so," Cherry admitted.

"You're welcome to have your supper with us," Jane offered, hoping against hope that Cherry would refuse and trying not to look too relieved when she did. She was also hoping that Copper would come to supper when she invited him, or she was going to get caught lying to save face.

"I expect Dad and I will go out and get something, when he gets home, like we do most nights," Cherry said uncomfortably.

"That will be nice."

"Jane, don't you care about him at all?" Cherry asked plaintively.

"I like him very much," Jane said at once. "He's a very nice man, and I owe him a lot."

Cherry felt sick. She managed a wan smile and made an excuse to go over to the small house where she and her father were staying.

When she was gone, Jane let go of the tears she'd been holding back and was just mopping herself up when Meg walked in with a tray of cookies and cake and tea, smiling.

The smile faded at once when she saw Jane's ravaged face. "Is she gone already? What in the world happened?"

Jane wiped savagely at the traces of tears. "Everything!" she raged. "That pirate! That cold-blooded, blond-headed snake!"

"Todd? Why are you mad at our accountant?"

"He's no accountant," Jane said viciously. "He's the head of a computer company and he's worth millions!"

Meg started, and then burst out laughing. "Oh, for heaven's sake, pull the other one!"

"It's true! He's got a Rolls at home!"

Meg set the tray down. "There, there, they were putting you on. Why, Todd's no millionaire!"

"He is," Jane insisted. "Cherry didn't want to agree with what her mother told me, but she did. Her mother might lie to me. Cherry never would."

Meg was less certain now. She frowned. "If he's a millionaire, why's he down here keeping your books?"

"Because I'm a poor cripple," Jane said huskily. "And he felt sorry for me. He's spending his vacation getting me out of the hole." She put her face in her hands and shook her head. "Now I don't have to wonder why the bank let me have the loan, either. I'm sure he stood good for it. I'll owe him my soul!"

Meg wiped her hands on her apron, hovering nervously. "Jane, you mustn't get upset like this. Wait until Todd gets back and talk to him about it."

"What will I tell him?"

"That you didn't know..."

"And now that I do?" she asked openly. "I'll tell him I know he's rich, and then he'll never be sure if I care for him or his wallet, will he? He might think I knew all along. His ex-wife said that he's been featured in all the business magazines. I don't read them, but he doesn't know that.''

''I see what you mean.''

Jane got up from the sofa. ''Well, I'm going to set his mind at ease, with a little help.''

''From whom?''

''Copper, of course,'' Jane said. ''He's already said that Copper and I seemed to be an item. Why shouldn't we be? Copper said he'd marry me in a minute if I was willing.''

''That's no reason to get married! Copper deserves better!''

Jane stared at her housekeeper. ''Of course he does, and it won't be for real. I'm going to ask an old friend for a favor, that's all.''

Meg relaxed. ''As long as he doesn't get hurt.''

''He won't.'' She didn't add that she would. She'd already been hurt. But Todd wasn't going to know. She was going to turn the tables on him and save her pride. It was the only thing she had left to protect herself with now.

As she'd guessed, Copper was willing to help her out by coming over to supper. He was on call, though, so he brought his beeper with him. They sat down to an early supper of fried chicken and vegetables. Jane was wearing a white dress and her hair was immaculately brushed back and secured with white combs. She looked elegant and very beautiful, except for the hollow expression in her eyes.

''Does it matter so much that he's got money?'' Copper asked her over coffee.

"It would to him, if he thought it was the reason I was attracted to him," she said.

"He'll know better."

"How?"

"He loves you, you idiot," Copper said curtly. "He'll be furious, and not at you. I don't doubt he'll have some choice words for his ex-wife."

"Maybe he'll thank her," she returned lightly. "After all, he was in a bit of a muddle here. He'd backed himself into a corner playing the part of a working man with no prospects."

"It probably meant more to him that you loved him in his disguise."

"How would he know that I hadn't been in on the secret all along?"

Copper nodded; it was a logical question. But he was smiling when he put down his napkin. "Because Cherry will tell him how shocked you were."

"Maybe I'm a good actress. Cherry's mother said that plenty of women had wanted him for his bank account."

"And don't you think he'd know the difference between a woman who wanted money and a woman who wanted him?"

"I don't know," Jane said honestly.

"Listen . . ."

The front door opened without even a knock and Todd stalked into the dining room. He was wearing a gray business suit with a spotless white shirt and a silk tie. His boots were hand-tooled leather. He was wearing a Rolex watch on his left wrist and a signet ring with a diamond that would have blinded a horse. For the first time, Jane saw him as he really was: an authority figure bristling with money and power.

He didn't smile as he stared at her, and his gaze didn't waver. "When Miss Emory finally got to me with Marie's message, I canceled a meeting. I was waiting for Marie when she got back home. I've had her version of what she said. Let's have yours."

Copper cleared his throat, to make sure that Todd knew he was sitting there.

Todd glanced at him with cold gray eyes. "I haven't missed the cozy supper scenario," he told the doctor. "But I know why it's being played out. Do you?"

"Oh, I have a dandy idea," Copper replied. "Wouldn't it have been easier all around to just tell the truth in the first place? Or were you having fun at Jane's expense?"

Todd laughed without mirth. He stuck his hands into his slacks pockets and stared at Jane from his superior, elegant height. "Fun. I've got merger negotiations stacked one on another, international contracts waiting for consideration, stockholders telephoning twice a day... No, I haven't been having fun. I've put my life on hold trying to get this horse ranch out of bankruptcy so that Jane would at least have a roof over her head. It was an impulse. Once I started the charade, I couldn't find a way to stop it."

"You could have told me the truth," Jane said stiffly.

"What truth?" he asked pleasantly. "That I felt sorry for you, because you were hurt and such a fighter despite your injuries? And that you stood to lose everything you owned just for lack of an accountant? I couldn't walk away.''

"Well, thanks for all you did," Jane replied, averting her eyes. "But now that you've got me on my feet, I can stay there all by myself."

"Sure you can," he agreed. "You've got a licensing contract and some decent stock to breed. You'll make it. You would have anyway, if Tim had been a little sharper in the math department. This is a first-class operation. All I did was pull the loose ends together. You're a born rancher. You've got what it takes to make this place pay, with a little help from Tim and Meg.''

The praise unsettled her, even as it thrilled her. At least he didn't think she was an idiot. That was something. But the distance between them was more apparent than ever now that she knew the truth about him.

She clasped her hands tightly out of sight in her lap. "And you?"

"I've got a business of my own to run," he said. "Cherry will start back to school soon. We'd have had to leave anyway, a little later than this, perhaps. Cherry owes you a lot for what you've taught her. She has a chance in rodeo now."

"Cherry is my friend. I hope she always will be."

"Cherry. But not me?"

She looked up into his eyes. "I'm grateful for what you did. But you must surely see that we live in different worlds." She sighed wearily. "I'm not cut out for yours, any more than you're cut out for mine. It's just as well that it worked out this way."

"You haven't tried," he said angrily.

"I'm not going to," was the quiet reply. "I like my life as it is. Exactly as it is. I'm very grateful for the help you gave me. I'll repay the loan."

His face hardened. "I never doubted that you would. I backed it. I didn't fund it."

She nodded. "Thank you."

His chest rose and fell heavily. He glared at Copper, because he could say none of what he wanted to say with the unwanted audience.

"Shall I leave?" Copper offered.

"Not on your life," Jane said shortly.

"Afraid of me?" Todd murmured with a mocking smile.

"There's nothing more to say," she replied. "Except goodbye."

"Cherry will be devastated," he said.

She drew in a breath. "Yes, I know. I'm sorry. I don't want to hurt her. But, it's the only thing to do."

He looked unapproachable. "Perhaps we see different things. If you'll have Tim phone me Monday morning, I'll explain to him what I've done. You need a business manager, unless you want to end up in the same financial tangle you started in."

"I know that. I'll take care of it."

"Then I'll say good night."

"I'm grateful for everything," Jane added stiffly.

He looked at her for a long moment. "Everything?" he said in a sensuous tone.

She colored. It seemed to be the reaction he'd wanted, because he laughed coldly, nodded to Coltrain and stalked out, closing the door behind him.

Copper stared at her. "You fool. Is pride worth more than he is to you?"

"At the moment, yes," she said icily. She was fighting tears and trying not to show it. "He's a pompous, hateful..."

"You shouldn't have forced this discussion on him before you had a couple of days to think about what you wanted to do," he said gently. "Impulses are very often regretted."

"Is that a professional opinion?" she asked angrily.

"Personal, professional, there isn't much difference," he replied. "You're going to be sorry that you didn't give him a chance to talk."

"I did," she said with wide, innocent eyes. "And he did."

"He defended himself. That's all he had time to do. With me sitting here, he hardly had the opportunity to do any real discussing."

"It's all for the best," she told him quietly.

"If you want to spend the rest of your life alone, maybe it is. But money isn't everything."

"When you don't have any, it is."

He glowered at her. "Listen to me, this might be the last chance you get. He's proud, too, you know. He won't come crawling back, any more than I would in his place. He's not the sort."

She knew that, too. She put her napkin on the table and stood up. "Thanks for coming over tonight. I don't think I'd have had the nerve to face him if you hadn't been here."

"What are friends for?" he asked. He stood up, too, and took her gently by the shoulders. "There's still time to stop him. You could go over to the cabin and have it out."

"We had it out," she argued.

"No, you didn't. You sat there like a polite hostess, but you sure as hell didn't do any discussing."

"I can take care of my own life, thank you."

"If that's true, what am I doing here?"

She searched his eyes. "Moral support."

He smiled. "I asked for that."

"I'm sorry. I really do appreciate your coming over so quickly when I asked."

"You're welcome. I hope you'll do the same for me if I'm ever in a comparable situation. But all you did was postpone the problem, you know. You didn't solve anything."

"I saved face," she replied. "He'll go back to Victoria and run his company, and I'll stay down here and breed horses and make money selling clothes."

"You'll be lonely."

She looked up. "That's nothing new. I was lonely before he came here. But people learn every day how to live with being lonely. I have a roof over my head, my books are in great shape, my body's healing nicely and I'm going to get this ranch back on its feet. It's what Dad would have wanted."

"Your dad would have wanted to see you happy."

She smiled. "Yes, but he was a realist. Todd wouldn't have married me," she said quietly. "You know it, too. I'm not the sort of woman rich men marry. I've got rustic manners and I don't know how to dress or use six forks for one meal."

"You could learn those things. You're beautiful, and elegant, and you have charm and grace. No woman born with a silver spoon could do better."

She grinned through her heartbreak. "You're a prince."

He sighed and checked his watch. "I'm done talking. I have to make rounds at the hospital. Call if you need me. But I wish you'd reconsider. You're not perfect. Why expect it of other people?"

"I never lied to him," she said pointedly. "In fact, I don't think I've ever really lied at all."

"You let him think we were romantically involved. That's lying."

"Implying," she corrected. "The rules don't say you can't imply things."

"I'll keep that in mind. I'll be in touch." He bent and kissed her cheek gently. "Try not to brood too much."

"I will."

She watched him go. The house was suddenly emptier than ever, and when she heard a car door slam minutes later, the whole world seemed that way. She peered through the curtains just in time to watch Todd and Cherry go down the driveway for the last time. The house they'd occupied was closed up and dark, like the cold space under her own heart.

Ten

Life became boring and tedious without Todd and Cherry, but the ranch prospered. Jane was a natural organizer. She discovered talents she hadn't ever realized she possessed, because her father had always taken care of the business end of the ranch. Now, she called breeders, made contacts, put ads in horse magazines and newspapers, faxed messages back and forth on sales and hired people to create sales catalogs for her. It was becoming second nature to handle things. Even Tim stood in awe of her.

The clothes licensing was also moving right along. The first of the television commercials had aired, and she was told that sales had shot up overnight. The commercials helped get her name in front of a larger segment of the public and helped in the stud operation. She was suddenly a household word. Despite the fact that she didn't like looking at herself on television and in print media ads, she had to admit that it was getting business.

But it was a lonely sort of life. She couldn't ride, although she'd tried once and ended up in bed for several days with a stiff and painful back. She could keep books, though, by using Todd's figures and backtracking to see how he'd arrived at them. While she was by no means his equal, she had a good head for figures and she picked up what was necessary very quickly. Life was good, but it was a lonely life. She wondered if Todd was glad to be gone out of her life.

In fact, some of Todd's employees wished that he would go out of their lives! Since his return to Victoria, nothing had been done right in any department he visited. The desks in the secretarial pool were sloppy. The new products division wasn't designing anything he liked. Furthermore, people weren't taking proper care of their floppy disks—he found one lying next to a cup of coffee on a desk. The marketing department wasn't out in the field enough selling new programs. And even Todd's secretary, the highly prized Miss Emory, was admonished about the state of her filing system when he went looking for a file and couldn't find it where he thought it should be.

It was no better at home. Cherry came in for criticism about the clothes she chose to wear to begin the next school year, her lack of attention to educational programming, and the certainty that she would end up in prison because she watched episodes of a popular adult cartoon on a music network. In fact, the first time he saw an episode of the cartoon, he called the cable company and had the channel that carried it taken out of his cable package.

Cherry was willing to go along with the understandable reaction—after all there was a generation gap. But when he canceled Cherry's horsemanship magazine after it featured an article on Jane, she felt that he was carrying things a bit too far.

"Dad," she ventured the week of the Victoria rodeo in which she was to compete, "don't you think you're getting just a little loopy lately?"

He glared at her over the top of his *Wall Street Journal.* "Loopy?"

"Overreacting. You know—canceling stuff." She cleared her throat at the unblinking glower she received. "Honestly, Dad, Miss Emory used a word I'll bet she never even thought until this week, after you grumbled about a letter she typed. And that's nothing to what Chris said when you threw his new computer program at him."

He put down the newspaper. "Is it my fault that people around me have suddenly forgotten how to do anything?" he asked curtly. "I have every right to expect good work from my employees. And you know why I canceled that garbage on television, not to mention that magazine . . ."

"Jane was in the magazine in two places," she said. "In a feature article, with color photos, and in a full-page ad. Didn't she look great?"

He averted his eyes. "I didn't notice."

"Really?" she asked. "Then why did you have the magazine open on your desk, where the photo was?"

He flapped the pages of his financial paper noisily. "Don't you have homework to do?"

"Dad, school hasn't started back yet."

He frowned. "Hasn't it?"

She got up out of her chair. "You could call her, you know."

"Call her!" He threw the paper down. His gray eyes flashed fire. "Call her, hell! She wouldn't even listen! She gave me all this *toro excretio* about different worlds and how . . . what are you laughing at?"

"Toro excretio?" she emphasized, giggling as she realized what the slang meant.

"I heard it from the wife of a concrete magnate," he said. "We sat on a committee together. Best description I ever heard. Anyway, don't change the subject."

"You could have tried to change Jane's mind."

"What would be the point?" he muttered. "She wanted to get married, until she found out who I was."

Cherry smiled. "That sounds nice. She'd certainly look lovely in high fashion, and I can't think of anyone who'd make a better stepmother."

"You've got a mother," he said harshly.

"We don't speak, haven't you noticed?" she asked coldly. "She hurt Jane."

He avoided her gaze. "Yes. Don't think I didn't give her my two cents' worth as well about that, but she's pregnant, I understand. She was emotional when she carried you."

"Maybe a new baby will make her happier."

"Ha!"

"Well, it will keep her occupied," Cherry continued. "What about Jane?"

"She's going to marry the cowboy doctor from hell and have little doctors, I guess," he muttered.

Cherry grinned. "Fat chance, when she's crazy about you. You're crazy about her, too. You just won't admit it. You'd rather roar around up here and drive everybody who works for you to using strong language or getting drunk on weekends."

"They don't do that!"

"Chris did, after you threw his program at him," Cherry informed him. "And he said that he was going to move out to California and help develop a virtual reality program for disgruntled employees so that they could turn their bosses into mud puddles and drop rocks in them."

"Vicious boy." He sighed. "I guess I'll have to give him a raise. God knows, he'd set virtual reality back twenty years."

She laughed. "And what about Jane?"

"Stop asking me that!"

"I'll bet she cries herself to sleep every night, thinking she's not good enough for you."

His face went very still. "What?"

"Well, that's what she thought. When Mom told her you were the head of a company and filthy rich, she went as white as a sheet. Mom made her feel bad about being a rancher and not reading intellectual magazines and not being upper crust."

"How dare she!" Todd said icily. "Jane's every bit as upper crust as your mother is!"

"Nobody told Jane that. She has a very low self-image."

"Stop talking like a psychologist."

"Merry's going to be one. She says I have a very good self-image."

"Nice of her."

"Anyway, Jane only has a high school education..."

"So do I, for God's sake!"

"...and she doesn't feel comfortable around high society people..."

"You know how I hate parties," he muttered.

"...and she thought you'd probably not want to have somebody like her in your life in a serious way."

"Of all the harebrained, idiotic, half-baked ideas! She's beautiful, doesn't she know that? Beautiful and kind and warm and loving." His voice grew husky with memory, and his body tingled with sweet memories. "She's everything a woman should be."

"The doctor sure thinks so," Cherry said with a calculating glance. "In fact, it wouldn't surprise me one bit if she didn't marry him on the rebound. He'd be over the moon. He's crazy about her."

His eyes narrowed. "She doesn't love him."

"Lots of people get married when they don't love each other. He's a good doctor. He can give her everything she wants, and they've always been good friends. I'll bet they'd make a wonderful marriage."

"Cherry...!"

"Well, Dad, that shouldn't bother you," she said pointedly. "After all, you don't want to marry her."

"The hell I don't!"

Cherry's eyebrows shot up. "You do?"

He hesitated, started to deny the impulsive outburst, and then settled into the chair with a heavy sigh. "Of course I do," he said harshly. "But it's too late. I wasn't honest with her at the beginning. I've made so many mistakes that I doubt she'd even talk to me now."

"If she loves you, she would."

"Sure," he scoffed. "The minute I call her up, she'll hang up. If she knows I'm coming to the ranch, she'll leave. I didn't spend several weeks there without learning something about her reactions."

Cherry puzzled over that. He was right. Jane would be like a whipped pup, eager to avoid any more blows.

Then she had a thought. "The rodeo," she said. "I'm going to compete in the rodeo, and Jane knows about it. Do you really think she'd miss watching me through my paces after all the time she put in on me?"

He pursed his lips, deep in thought. "No. But she'll disguise herself."

"Probably."

"And she'll sit as far away as possible."

"That, too." She grinned. "You could ask Chris to sit in the audience up on the top of the stands and watch out for her."

"Chris would sell me down the river . . ."

"Not if you give him that raise."

He groaned. "The things I don't do for you!"

"We'll all live happily ever after," Cherry said smugly. "After you grovel enough to Jane and convince her that you can make her happy."

"I'm not groveling."

She grinned. "Have it your way."

"I'm not!"

She left him protesting and went over to Merry's house to watch television.

Tim and Meg had a light supper with Jane the afternoon of the Victoria rodeo. She sat there deep in thought, picking at her food, as usual, and not talking, also as usual.

"Are you going up to Victoria to watch Cherry compete?" Tim asked her.

She glowered at him. "No. *He'll* be there."

"Of course he will, he's her father."

She stabbed a piece of carrot. "I'd like to watch her. But I don't want to run into him."

"You could wear a scarf and dark glasses," Meg advised. "And a dress. You never wear dresses. He wouldn't recognize you. Especially if you sat way up in the stands. He'll be right down front where Cherry is."

Jane thought about that. Meg was right. That's exactly where he'd be. She dropped the piece of carrot into her mouth and chewed it. "I guess I could do that. There'll be a huge crowd. Anyway, I doubt if he'll even look for me."

"Well, of course he would..." Tim argued.

Meg kicked him under the table and he winced.

"I mean, of course he wouldn't," Tim amended.

Jane glanced at him and then at Meg. "Are you two up to something?"

"My goodness, no," Meg said easily and smiled. "But it would be nice to know how Cherry did in the competition. We watched her practice, day after day."

That would explain their interest. "I guess I might go up for the barrel racing, if Tim can drive me," Jane said.

"Sure I can. Meg can come, too."

"I'd love to," Meg agreed. Jane missed the relief on Meg's features that was quickly erased.

"We'd better get a move on, then," Jane said after a glance at her watch. "It will take us a little while to get there, and there's sure to be a crowd."

She pulled on a simple green-and-white cotton sundress, with sandals and a white cardigan. She put up her long blond hair and tied a scarf over it and then secured a pair of dark glasses over her eyes.

Meg walked past the door and looked in.

"Will it do?" Jane asked, turning toward her.

"It's perfect," Meg assured her, and went on down the hall.

Jane nodded at her reflection. Nobody would recognize her in this getup, she concluded.

She might not have been so confident if she'd heard Meg on the telephone in her quarters a couple of minutes later, telling Cherry every detail of Jane's disguise, as they'd already conspired.

"I feel guilty," Meg said.

"Never you mind," Cherry replied. "It's all for a good cause. Think how miserable Jane and Dad are going to be if we don't do something!"

"Jane's lost weight."

"Dad's lost weight *and* employees," Cherry murmured dryly. "If he keeps on like this, some of the people in his software development department are going to stuff him into a computer and ship him overseas. This has just got to work. I'll see you both tonight."

"Good luck, honey," Meg said with genuine affection. "We'll all be rooting for you."

"Thanks. I think I'm going to need all the help I can get. But knowing that Jane is in the stands will do me more good than anything."

"She'll be there. Don't you worry."

Meg hung up and went to meet Jane in the hall. "Goodness, you certainly do look different!" she said.

"I feel different. Now all I have to do is sit far enough away so that nobody recognizes me."

"Your own dad, God rest his soul, wouldn't recognize you like that," Meg said dryly.

"Well, hopefully Todd won't," Jane murmured, adjusting the scarf. "I have no wish whatsoever to get into any more arguments with him. But I can't miss seeing Cherry ride. I hope she wins."

"So do we," Tim agreed.

They drove up to Victoria in the truck. Riding was much easier for Jane since the pain in her back had eased. The damage was repairing itself and the pain only came now when she did stupid things—like trying to gallop on horseback.

It had been a bitter blow to realize that her rodeo days were over, but she was dealing with that. If only she could deal half as well with the sorrow that losing

Todd had caused her. Not a day went by when she didn't long for him.

He wouldn't feel that way about her, she was certain. A man with so much wealth and status wouldn't want an ordinary rancher from south Texas. Not when he could have movie actresses or top models or high-powered business executives. Having seen Marie, so poised and capable and able to run her own business, she had some idea of the sort of woman who appealed to Todd. And Jane was not that type.

It was more than likely that Marie had told the truth: Todd had only taken the job on an impulse because he felt sorry for Jane. He'd been kind, in his way, but she didn't need his pity. The best thing she could do now was to stay out of his way and not spoil Cherry's big night.

Cherry would be the one to suffer, if they had another argument, and Jane thought the girl had been hurt enough already.

Cherry wrote to her, though, and she wrote back. It wasn't as if they'd parted in anger. But Todd complicated that tenuous friendship. Jane was fairly certain that he didn't approve of his daughter's friendship with Jane, and it was a fair bet that Marie didn't.

When they arrived at the arena the parking lot was almost full. The floodlights were silhouetted against the dark sky and the opening ceremonies had already begun.

They got their tickets and then Jane made her way very carefully to the top rung of the spectator section, leaving Meg and Tim down front. She sat apart from the other few people, but she noticed a young man giving her covert looks. If he was a masher, she mused, he had a long way to fall. He'd better keep his distance.

She settled into her seat. The light cardigan felt good, because there was a slight nip in the summer night air. She sighed and worked to keep her mind on the people in the arena. But all it really wanted to do was think about Todd. Her heart raced at the thought that he was here, somewhere, in this very place. She was close to him again, even if he didn't know it. How wonderful it felt to know that.

There was competition after competition. She sat through bareback bronc riding, steer riding, steer wrestling and calf roping. The competitors were narrowed down as man after man failed to meet the time limit. Prizes were awarded. And then, finally, the barrel-racing competition was announced and the first rider was out of the gate.

Cherry was fourth. An excited Jane sat on the edge of her seat. Part of her mourned because she would never compete again. But her heart raced, her blood surged as she watched Cherry go through her paces, watched the girl match the best time Jane had ever done. There were cheers when Cherry rode out of the arena. Jane felt the sting of tears in her eyes as she knew, deep inside, that nobody was going to beat Cherry tonight. All the hard work and practice and patience had paid off. She felt as if she were in the saddle with her protégé. It was a wonderful feeling— the sort a parent might have, pride in a child.

It was no surprise at all when the winner was announced, and it was Cherry. Jane watched her accept her trophy as flashbulbs went off, and her proud father gave her a warm hug from the sidelines.

Todd! Jane watched him with an ache that went all the way to her toes. She'd been in his arms, too. She knew how it felt, but in a different way than a daughter would. She was empty inside, an outsider looking into a warm family circle that she could never share.

It was time to go. She got up from her seat and carefully made her way down to the seats where she'd left Tim and Meg, but they were nowhere in sight. Perhaps they'd gone to congratulate Cherry, something Jane would love to have done, but she didn't dare. Not with Todd so close.

With a sigh of pure longing, she went toward the place where they'd left the truck, but she must have forgotten its exact position. She couldn't seem to find it.

While she was standing among the dark vehicles, searching, there was a sound nearby and she was suddenly picked up in hard, warm arms that felt all too familiar.

Her eyes met gray ones in a set face as she was carried toward a waiting black Ferrari.

"Take off those damn glasses," Todd said curtly.

She fumbled them away from her wide, shocked blue eyes. "How did you . . . ?"

"Cherry conspired with Tim and Meg," he replied, turning toward his car.

"Where are they?"

"At the house, waiting for us." He met her eyes as he reached the car. "They're going to have a long wait," he added sensuously. "We have some lost time to make up."

"Now, you just wait a minute," she began.

"I've waited too damn long already," he breathed as his mouth lowered onto hers and stilled every word in her mouth and every thought in her whirling brain.

She faltered, trying to decide how to save her pride.

"Give up," he whispered. "Kiss me."

"I can't... We don't... It wouldn't—" she murmured dizzily.

"You can, we do, and it *will* work," he said on a husky laugh. "We're going to get married and raise several more cowgirls and maybe even a cowboy or two."

"You don't want to marry someone like me," she said sadly.

"Yes," he told her, his loving eyes on her face. "I want to marry someone exactly like you, a woman who has a heart as beautiful as her face and body, a woman who loves me and my daughter fiercely. I want you, Jane. Now and forever."

She couldn't believe it was really happening. She looked into his eyes and sailed among the stars.

"I see dreams in your eyes," he said softly. "Marry me, and I'll make them all come true, every one."

"I'm not educated..."

"Neither am I." He kissed her hungrily before he opened the door.

"I'm not sophisticated," she persisted.

"Neither am I." He put her into the passenger seat and carefully belted her in.

"I can't stand high society parties..."

"Neither can I." He closed her door and got in beside her.

"Todd..."

He cranked the powerful engine, reversed the car, eased it out of the parking lot and headed for open country. His hand found hers after he'd shifted into the final gear, and he held on tight.

"I've been lonely. Have you?" he asked.

"Lonelier than I ever knew I could be," she said, capitulating.

"I wanted to telephone you, or come to see you, but I knew you wouldn't listen. You're as proud as I am."

"Sadly, yes."

"But we'll manage to get along, most of the time. And after we argue, we'll make up."

She smiled, leaning her head on his shoulder. "Oh, yes."

"And Cherry will be the happiest girl in her class when school starts in Jacobsville."

"Are we going to live in Jacobsville?" she asked with a start.

"Of course. I haven't finished saving the ranch yet," he said dryly.

"Oh, I see. So that's it. You want my ranch, you blackhearted villain," she accused and ruined it with a giggle.

"Yes, I do," he said fervently. "Because without me, you'll end up right back in the red again. You'll forget to use purchasing orders for supplies, you'll get the figures in the wrong columns, you'll forget to keep proper receipts for taxes..."

"Actually," she said sheepishly, "I've already done all those things."

"God help me!"

"Now, now. I'm sure you'll get us in the black again in no time," she said, making a mental note to mess up her accounts before he took a look at them. "After all, you did start a computer company all by yourself."

He glowered at her. "It was easier than trying to run a ranch, all things considered. At my business, people do what I tell them to."

"I'll do what you tell me to. Some of the time," she replied.

"That's what I was afraid of."

She closed her eyes. "I'll make you like it."

He chuckled and drew her close. "Of course you will."

Halfway home, he found a small dirt track and pulled the car onto it, under some trees. He turned off the engine and turned to Jane. He held his arms out and she went into them.

Turbulent minutes later, he lifted his head. Her eyes in the dim light were sparkling with emotion like blue sapphires and she was clinging to him, trembling faintly as his lean hand smoothed softly over her bare breasts.

"We have to go home," he whispered reluctantly.

"Are you sure?" She reached up and kissed him hungrily.

He groaned, but he pulled back just a fraction of an inch. "Not really. But this isn't wise."

"Why not?"

He glanced in the rearview mirror with a rueful smile and quickly rearranged her disheveled clothing. "Because the local sheriff's department has deputies with no romance in their souls."

"How do you . . ." The flashing lights behind them caught her eye, and she made a shocked sound as a tall man came up to the driver's side of the car and knocked.

A resigned Todd let the window down and grinned at the unsmiling uniformed man. "I know, this is the wrong place for what we were doing. But our daughter and several other people are congregated in our living room at home, and there's no privacy anywhere!"

The uniformed man looked from Jane to Todd and made an amused sound deep in his throat. "I know what you mean. My wife and I have four kids and they never leave the house. Lot of garbage, that talk about teenagers always being on the go. All mine want to do is play video games and eat pizza."

"I know just what you mean."

"All the same," the deputy said wryly, "this really isn't . . ."

"The best place. I get the idea." Todd grinned again. "Okay. We'll go home."

"Rent them a movie," he suggested. "Works for my brood. You put on one of those new thrillers and they won't even know if you're still in the house."

"That's the best idea yet. Thanks!"

He smiled. "My wife and I have been married twenty-six years," he said with a chuckle. "You wouldn't believe some of the diversions we've come up with to keep them busy. Have a nice evening." He touched the brim of his hat and went back to his car.

"You let him think we were married," she accused gently.

"Why not, when we will be by the end of the week," he said warmly. "I can't wait."

She slid her hand into his when he cranked the car and started to reverse it. "Neither can I."

They were married a few days later, with Tim and Meg as witnesses and Cherry as maid of honor. It was a quiet ceremony in Jacobsville, with no one except the four of them. Afterward, they all went out to eat at Jacobsville's best restaurant and then Todd and Jane flew down to Jamaica for a very brief honeymoon before school started.

Despite their need for each other, they'd been very circumspect until the vows were spoken. But no sooner were they installed in their room overlooking the bay in their luxurious Montego Bay hotel suite when Todd picked her up and tossed her onto the king-size bed, following her down before she had time to get her breath.

"Oh, but we really should... go and look... at the ocean," she teased as he brushed lazy, sensuous kisses on her parted lips.

"Indeed we should." His lean hand smoothed down her body, kindling sharp desires, awakening nerves. She gasped and shivered when he trespassed under the thin elastic of her briefs. "Do you want to go now?" he whispered into her mouth as his hand moved exploringly.

She moaned.

He laughed softly, moving his mouth to the soft curve of her breasts under the scoop-neck knit top. "That's what I thought."

In no time at all, they were both nude, twisting against each other in a fever of deprived need. He urgently drew her into the taut curve of his body, but even then he was tender, fitting her to him in a silence punctuated with the soft gasps of pleasure that he drew from her mouth with each glorious lunge of his body as it worked its way hungrily into hers.

He nibbled at her mouth while his hand, curved over her upper thigh, drew her insistently to meet the rhythm of his powerful body.

He lifted his head to watch her reactions from time to time, and despite the glitter of his eyes and the sharp drag of his breathing, he seemed totally in control. On the other hand, she was sobbing and shivering, clinging desperately to him as the sensations, which were still so new to her, flung her body to and fro against his in waves of hot pleasure.

She arched into him violently, and his hand contracted. "Gently," he whispered. "We have to be careful of your back."

"Gen . . . tly?" she groaned. "Oh, Todd . . . I'm . . . dying!" She pushed against him again, following the trail of the pleasure that had grasped her so viciously just seconds before.

"Here, then." He guided her, watching until he saw her response quicken. He smiled through his own tension as he gave her the ecstasy she pleaded for. Her eyes widened and went black with shock as she stiffened and then convulsed under his delighted gaze.

She felt the tears slide from her eyes as oblivion carried her to heights she'd never dreamed of scaling. And then, just when she was returning to her body, she saw him laugh and then groan as he pushed against her and shuddered with his own satisfaction.

He fell heavily against her, his heartbeat shaking him, and rolled to his side with her clasped against him. One long leg wrapped around her, drawing her even closer while he worked to breathe.

"If it keeps getting better," she whispered into his throat, "I think it may kill me."

He chuckled. "Both of us."

"You laughed," she accused softly.

He lifted his damp head and looked into her eyes, smiling. "Oh, yes." He traced her mouth. "With shock and pleasure and the glory of loving and being loved while I made love. I've never felt so complete before."

She smiled shyly. "Neither have I. Even though it was good the first time."

He kissed her softly. "We'll have years and years of this, and children, and challenges to keep us fit. And I'll love you until I die," he added fervently.

She pressed closer. "I'll love you just as long!" She closed her eyes. "Even longer."

He made a contented sound and bent to kiss her soft mouth. But very quickly the tenderness grew stormy and hungry, and she rolled into his arms again, as hungry as he.

Later, lying in Todd's arms as the morning sun silvered the bed, she thought that she'd never been happier or more fulfilled in her whole life. Or more weary.

"Exhausted already?" he exclaimed when she shifted in his arms and groaned as her sore muscles protested. "I'll have to feed you more oysters!"

"I'll feed you to the oysters if you don't let me sleep," she teased, nuzzling closer. "I know we agreed that it would be nice to start our family right away, but I'll die of fatigue before we get to the first one at this rate!"

He chuckled and kissed her forehead softly. "We'll sleep a bit longer, then. Happy?" he murmured drowsily.

"Happier than I ever dreamed I could be."

"And your back . . . is it all right?"

"It's fine. Actually, I think this is therapeutic for it."

"All the more reason to exercise it twice a day."

She kissed his bare shoulder. "Later. I've had no sleep in two days. I kept thinking that your ex-wife would find some way to sabotage the ceremony."

"That wasn't likely," he said with a weary grin. "Cherry had made several threats. I think she's going to be a very formidable surgeon when she gets out of medical school. Anyone who can buffalo Marie shouldn't have any trouble with hospital staff."

Jane smiled. "She and her mother do get along better now, at least."

"Oh, Marie learned her lesson the hard way. If she isn't nice to you, she'll lose her daughter. That's the one thing that made her apologize to you, and it's kept her pleasant." He stretched lazily. "She even offered to redecorate the ranch house for you free after she has the baby."

"I'll think about that."

"I had a feeling that's what you'd say. She means well."

"I know. I love you."

He smiled. "I love you."

He drew her close and pulled the sheet up over them. In the distance, the crash of the surf was like a watery serenade. Jane closed her eyes and turned her face into Todd's chest. And her dreams were sweet.

* * * * *

SILHOUETTE® *Desire*

COMING NEXT MONTH

#919 MR. EASY—Cait London

April's *Man of the Month*, Wyatt Remington, wasn't ready to reveal his true identity to his long-lost daughter. But could he convince *her* boss, sexy Tallulah Ames, that he really didn't have a thing for younger women?

#920 THE PERFECT FATHER—Elizabeth Bevarly

From Here to Maternity

Seductive Sylvie Venner thought she'd found the perfect candidate for the father of her baby—he was honest, hardworking and handsome! But Chase Buchanan had no plans of ever becoming a dad....

#921 MISS LIZZY'S LEGACY—Peggy Moreland

Callie Benson didn't want Judd Barker's help to discover who her great-great-grandmother was. After all, the hard-hearted man was too sexy for *her* own good!

#922 BEACH BABY—Karen Leabo

Isabel DeLeon needed a husband so she could adopt the abandoned baby she'd found on the beach. Unfortunately, a husband was the one thing Craig Jaeger swore he would never be....

#923 THE MADDENING MODEL—Suzanne Simms

Hazards, Inc.

Sunday Harrington was beautiful, brainy...and Simon Hazard found her unbearable—until the pair got stranded in the jungle and he learned that there was more to her than met the eye.

#924 ERRANT ANGEL—Justine Davis

Spellbound

No way did loner Dalton MacKay want a do-gooder like Evangeline Law thinking she could change his brooding ways. But the more time he spent with the beautiful angel, the harder it was to push her away....

MILLION DOLLAR SWEEPSTAKES (III)

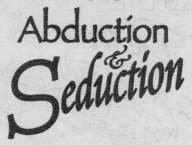